CHASING SHADOWS
GENESIS

CHASING SHADOWS
GENESIS

ZACHARIAH JONES

WATER SIGN BOOKS

WATER SIGN BOOKS

Published by Water Sign Books
Stillwater, Minnesota 55082, USA

Copyright © 2022 by Water Sign Books

All rights reserved

Library of Congress Control Number: 2022910803

ISBNs:
979-8-98-634400-3 (hardcover)
979-8-98-634401-0 (paperback)
979-8-9863440-2-7 (eBook – Kindle)
979-8-9863440-3-4 (eBook – iBook)
979-8-9863440-4-1 (eBook)

Chasing Shadows is a work of fiction. Names, character, places, and incidents are the product of the author's imagination or are used fictitiously, and any resemblance to actual persons, living or dead, businesses, companies, events, or locales is entirely coincidental.

Cover art by Nicholas Alexander Xayne

Set in Saint Paul, Minnesota ~ 1924

*For my friends and family who have gone before me
and those that have yet to arrive*

Chasing Shadows
Genesis

Noisome (adjective): offensive to the senses and especially to the sense of smell

~ MERRIAM-WEBSTER DICTIONARY

CHAPTER 1
Union Depot

December 20, 1924, 4:18 p.m.

The whistle from the engine car sounded as Jarek felt the train begin to slow. The long journey from New York City to Saint Paul was finally coming to a close. What seemed like almost a month of travel was actually less than a week. It seemed to Jarek that the train arrived later than it did because it was so dark outside the windows. He could tell it was a bitter temperature outside the comfort of the passenger car. Peering through the small window, the dark-haired young man could see steam rising from the manhole covers in the streets beyond the train rails. Small flakes of snow were coming down slowly from the sky. The snow drifting down, combined with the frosty air, gave Jarek a calming yet chilling feeling. He had felt so much unease over the past month, so it was refreshing to just sit and observe out the window as the train continued its arrival in this growing city along the Mississippi River. Jarek pulled out his pocket watch. There was ample time to find some dinner at a local establishment and still arrive at the O'Connell residence before getting too late into the evening.

As Jarek sat in the train car, the unease began to creep back into his thoughts. He traveled here on his own accord. However, the travel was significantly prodded by the letters he received requesting help, and his own intuition was nudging him to act upon the request.

Jarek always knew he was different, and several of those close to him were aware he was unique. Even some strangers in New York were aware of his gifts because he had helped others when he could. Word must have spread about his abilities beyond New York. Sometimes people unknown to him would seek him out asking for his help, or he would be drawn to strangers who needed his gift. Those strangers were always from New York, so when he began to sense something was off, and then two separate letters arrived, he knew something bigger was happening.

The train came to a halt, and the passengers began to stand from their seats and grab their belongings. Jarek sat waiting for the other passengers to compile their belongings and exit the passenger car before getting up. Though he was anxious to get off the train and stretch his legs, he knew it wasn't proper as a younger man to barge in front of those older than him and the women traveling alone. Jarek secured his belongings once the car was nearly empty and moved to the train platform.

The air felt brisk, with a slight breeze tunneling through the tall buildings in this growing downtown. There was a hint of moisture in the air adding to the chill and creating some fog that gave shivers to people exiting the train. Clearly, many of the passengers were not prepared for the weather. Though Jarek had never been anywhere but the East Coast, he knew to dress appropriately. However, it was still a sharper sting to his face than he was anticipating.

Chasing Shadows ~ Genesis

As he was walking into the train depot to ask for directions, he couldn't help but feel the energies surrounding him. He was getting feelings of happiness and excitement. Jarek had been to towns in his past that only felt dark and hopeless, especially during the Great War. So he had a sense of relief that this city seemed to have many good-natured people and minimal impact by dark entities. He knew not to take this for granted, as he knew there was something dark awaiting him in this city.

Saint Paul Union Depot was an immaculate structure, clearly not that old. It had nearly a dozen different train platforms of people coming and going from the bustling city. Thankfully, Jarek overheard someone say there was an establishment right inside the depot to eat some food. Above the door, when walking into the depot, he noticed a large clock with the time. The depot was crowded with people, just as much as outside on the platform.

A grand Christmas tree at least twenty feet tall was at the center of the large open room. Garlands and elaborate ornaments adorned many of the doorways, windows, and ticket windows. A string ensemble playing familiar carols overshadowed the hustle and bustle of people. Jarek always appreciated this time of year. No matter what darkness came through the veil or entities tried to capitalize on the long dark nights, he knew there was always hope and comfort in the season.

Jarek walked up to the eatery and sat down at a small two-person table. He removed his coat and hat, and placed them on the back of his chair. He set his suitcase and satchel down on the floor before taking a seat. It was fairly busy, but a man younger than himself came over to greet him.

"Good evening, welcome to Saint Paul Union Depot, sir. We have beef roast or creamed chicken as our entrée options tonight, and it comes with a side of boiled potatoes. After all, most everything comes with a side of boiled potatoes here," the young man said with a smirk.

"Excuse me?" Jarek asked him, genuinely confused by the comment.

"Oh, I'm sorry. It is a jest we have here. See, this is the Saint Paul Union Depot. Ever since the workmen started constructing this building, they nicknamed it SPUD," he said, continuing with his smirk. "So we serve everything with boiled potatoes. It is not that funny to travelers passing through, but it amuses us here."

"I understand it now. I am sorry. I have just had a very long travel from New York City to here. The witticism passed right over me. I will take the beef roast . . . with the side of boiled potatoes," Jarek said as he smiled at the waiter.

"Sounds wonderful, sir. I am easily amused at times. I do apologize. Oh, and welcome to Saint Paul! Dreadful time of year to visit, if you aren't used to the cold."

"No need to apologize. As I said, I am just tired from the long train ride."

"I will return as quickly as I can with your meal. Would you like a coffee or hot tea to help warm you up?"

"Yes, please, coffee would be perfect . . ." Jarek was responding to the young man when suddenly he felt a presence coming near him.

"I will be right back with that, sir," the young man said as he backed away from the table, turned, and walked toward the kitchen.

Not a moment sooner than when the young man turned, the other chair at the table cantered ever so slightly. Jarek could see a very subtle depression form in the cushion on the seat. Jarek knew better than to talk openly to a spirit in a crowded place such as this for two reasons. First, the people passing by would assume him wrong in the head. Secondly, spirits could change disposition quickly and could, in fact, cause damage or a ruckus with people. This entity didn't feel malevolent, so he let it be for now, but he was unsure of why he stayed completely hidden from Jarek's sight.

Jarek continued to stare at the chair, attempting to read the situation better, as the young man from the eatery brought him his hot coffee.

"This should help take some of the chill out of the air for you," he said as he placed the cup in front of Jarek. "I will be back with your dinner shortly."

"Thank you. May I ask you for some directions to the neighborhood I am traveling to this evening? Or at least get me in the general direction?"

"Of course, what neighborhood are you looking for?"

"It is the home of Martin O'Connell, on Saint Claire Street—" He barely finished the sentence before the young man interrupted.

"The O'Connell mansion? You mean Mr. O'Connell, who owns the printing press? Gee, he is lousy with money. One of the richest men in the city, I reckon. It's a pity what happened there this year . . ." he said, trailing off. "I'm sorry, sir. Sometimes I keep talking when I mean to keep those thoughts to myself."

"No need, mac, I only know the general situation surrounding what happened. I was asked to visit to help the family through this time. Though to be honest, the only thing I know is the mother has died, and the family is having a hard time handling it."

"Are you some type of minister? I didn't think that the O'Connell family was very religious, but I suppose in a situation like this, someone might find God."

"No, no, I am not a minister. I've just been asked to help guide them and find closure in the situation, I believe. Do you know of the details? Of course, anything you'd be willing to share that isn't gossip."

"I know they are still hunting the bastard that murdered Mrs. O'Connell. They found her in the library on the second floor, I heard . . . Her body was pretty mutilated, I heard, too. Mr. O'Connell hasn't been seen much since, except at the printing factory. Just Mr. O'Connell, his daughter, and their governess remain in the house. I know a few employees still work there, but many quit after the incident. My cousin was their carriage boy, but he left a few weeks back, saying the whole situation was too gruesome and the governess was very difficult to work with."

He seemed to take a pause, as to not seem to be gossiping.

"I know I shouldn't say so much. After all, I can only go by what people are saying."

"That is all right. I am glad you shared with me. It helps bring to light some of the concerns. It is never all right for anyone to have to go through a situation like the one you just described."

"However, sir, to get to the home is fairly simple. Leave out the main exit of the Union Depot, walk to Fourth Street, and go left. You will see the Cathedral of Saint Paul; just keep walking toward that. Before getting to the church, you will come across Saint Claire Street. Go left and walk a few blocks down. On the right you will see the mansion. Can't be more than a twenty- to thirty-minute walk. The mansion has one grand tower on the right side at least four stories tall, and there is a stunning statue in the yard of some mythical creature . . . part man, part goat . . ."

"Pan," Jarek interrupted.

"Excuse me?"

"It is probably a statue of the Greek god Pan." I have seen them before in yards in New York City."

"Nice to know! Anyway, you should find it. Just follow those directions. I'll go get your food. It should be ready by now."

The young man turned back to the kitchen, leaving Jarek alone with the spirit.

The chair next to Jarek cantered again ever so slightly. Someone going about their business would never have noticed. Jarek continued to sip his coffee and didn't make verbal contact with the spirit, but he knew what it needed.

The young man returned promptly and set down the plate of food on the table for Jarek.

"Thank you," Jarek said, nodding his head in appreciation. He had forgotten how famished he was until he could smell the beef roast in front of him.

"You're welcome, sir. Enjoy."

Jarek began to eat his dinner. He was eating rather quickly because he was very hungry but also because he did not want to arrive at the O'Connell house too late into the evening.

While he continued to eat, the spirit joining him at his table began to communicate with him. Not an audible communication in any manner, but it proceeded to talk with Jarek in his mind. It was as Jarek suspected—it was simply a spirit in need. It needed its story brought to light. The spirit was drawn to Jarek and knew that he would be able to help him.

Before he knew it, Jarek was finished with his plate of food—every bit eaten. The young man from the eatery came over to his table.

"Is there anything else I can assist you with before you venture out into the cold to the O'Connell mansion?"

"No, you have been a magnificent help. Thank you so much for the directions."

"You are most certainly welcome. I do hope you are able to help that family. They certainly need it. Whatever it is you really do . . . Well, I hope you can help them." The young man paused. "You can leave payment on the table. Ninety-five cents will cover the costs."

"Thank you," Jarek said to him as the young man walked away.

Quickly, Jarek opened his satchel and pulled out money to leave on the table. Then he tore a page out of his journal and began to scratch a note on it. Once he had finished, he gathered up his items. He put his hat and coat back on, nodded to the empty chair, and started heading toward the north exit of Union Station.

When he was only about twenty feet from the doorway, he turned and looked back toward the table he was sitting at. Next to the table was a man standing, staring at Jarek. He was wearing workman's overalls, looked to be mid-forties, and looked to be fairly mangled in injuries. He had a look of sadness and loneliness, yet there was a glimmer of appreciation as he stared at Jarek.

Soon the young man from the eatery approached the table and began to read the note Jarek left. Jarek turned and exited the Saint Paul Union Depot and headed toward Fourth Street.

Dear Sir,

Thank you so much for the dinner of beef roast. The boiled potatoes were exceptionally delicious. I need to ask a favor of you. Please do not share with others that I am visiting the O'Connell household. During this sensitive time for them, I do not wish to have other stressors on the family.

Also, I have a message for the overseer of SPUD. I have a story and request of him. While this structure was having some repairs several weeks back, a man was working on the cables within the lift shaft. At some point, he had to crawl to the base of the shaft and work on some of the mechanical systems. While he was working, the lift was lowered down on top of him by mistake. This resulted in injuring him badly, and he was unable to make much noise due to his chest being crushed. Once the lift was brought up off him, he was able to crawl to an opening off to the side but died shortly after.

He was a transient worker from Chicago. He is very sorry for some of the decisions he made in life, for drinking too much, and is sorry to the people he has hurt. He made a terrible mistake just to be able to buy more alcohol. He is regretful of so many things, but it is too late now, and he is ready to move on from this world.

He wishes for his body to be recovered from the opening near the lift and given a proper burial. His name was Michael Stafford, and he wishes for someone to contact his mother in Chicago—Ethel Stafford. She lives near Grant Park. He would like her to know that he has passed on so she can stop worrying. Her son is at rest now.

—*J. V.*

CHAPTER 2

ARRIVAL

December 20, 1924, 5:58 p.m.

Once Jarek stepped outside the SPUD, he quickly remembered how cold the air felt hitting his cheeks. The slight breeze felt like small sewing needles puncturing his skin, over and over. He looked around again, taking in the sight of this busy downtown. The tall buildings, the bustling streets, the snow coming down with the gentle wind—it was a beautiful sight. It seemed almost like a smaller version of New York City during the Christmas season, he thought to himself.

Jarek did not want to be away from the few family members and friends he had in New York during this time, but he knew there was something about the O'Connell family that was calling to him for help.

Jarek started walking north toward the street directly in front of the Union Depot and immediately saw a sign reading FOURTH STREET.

He took a left and headed west. It only took him a few blocks worth of walking before he saw a grand cathedral with an impressive dome. This had to be one of the largest churches he had ever seen. That clearly had to be the correct landmark the young man from the eatery was referencing, so Jarek kept walking toward it.

The snow was starting to fall from the sky at a faster rate, so quickly that it was beginning to accumulate on Jarek's hat and shoulders. Everyone on the walkways started to walk more quickly in an effort to reach their destinations before it got too treacherous to walk.

Everyone who passed by Jarek gave a slight nod or proper greeting. This caught him a bit off guard, because back home in New York City, everyone was "too busy" to even be friendly, it seemed. Internally, Jarek was hoping this was an indication that his greeting at the O'Connell household would not be completely unwelcomed. After all, he knew that his arrival to a stranger's home would be awkward enough. Jarek assumed that only one occupant was expecting him, whoever the person who sent the letters was.

Shortly before reaching the grounds of the cathedral, Jarek came to the intersection of Fourth Street and Saint Claire Street. Before turning left to continue on toward the mansion, he paused to look at the magnitude and elegance of the cathedral. He could hear the church choir rehearsing inside for their upcoming Christmas mass, no doubt. He saw an older couple having a conversation while seated on a snow-covered bench under a lamppost on the church lawn, and the snow coming down on the trees and statues scattered throughout was calming and mesmerizing. Jarek stood there enjoying everything this moment had to offer.

After a bit of time passed, there was a slight movement in Jarek's peripheral vision near an angel statue not too far off the walk where he was standing. He knew it was best to never turn your head quickly to look at shadows you see in the corner of your eye. This quick movement results in the very spirit trying to gain your attention to leave.

Jarek stood there looking directly at the church while slowly trying to focus on what entity was to his left near the statue. As he concentrated, it soon became the figure of a person, and it seemed to be looking directly toward him. It was simply a shadowy figure, which made making out details of the entity nearly impossible. As he slowly began to turn his head to try to make contact, the apparition vanished like a mist.

Jarek knew that beings such as this are oftentimes the remnants of someone who once walked the Earth. They were usually here to pass along a message to a loved one, or a part of them happened to cross back into this world by accident through a ripple of the veil. This type of spirit activity was typically at its peak during this time of year. Jarek knew this to be the case because of his own experiences and after some research. Winter solstice is at the core of this fact. Once it became harvest season through late winter, the days were at their darkest. The days around winter solstice were the shortest, with the longest nights. These long dark nights allow for the barrier of the veil to be at its thinnest, and oftentimes spirits, human and otherwise, were more likely to mistakenly cross into the world of the living. However, some spirits knew this, and they waited for the right time to move into this world. Those tended to be the darkest and most malevolent beings.

Nevertheless, this entity left before Jarek could attempt an interaction with it, so Jarek barely let it phase him since it was a common occurrence. He pulled out his pocket watch and saw it was nearly 6:30 p.m. He took a breath and continued on his journey down Saint Claire Street toward the O'Connell mansion.

Jarek continued to walk for several blocks, enjoying the snow and admiring the beauty of the homes here. He finally approached his destination. Based on the description the young man from SPUD had given him, Jarek knew it was the O'Connell home immediately.

The home stood high on a small hill, inset a ways off the street, with massive towering evergreen trees surrounding the sides and back of the property. The magnitude of the structure impressed Jarek. The home was built of brick, a full three stories tall, with a tower standing four stories tall near the small front porch. In the foreground, to the right of the main entrance, was the statue of the Greek god Pan that the young man from the eatery recalled. There was a drive that looped around to the back of the home, likely for the servants' entrance and carriage house, Jarek thought to himself.

The entire property was giving Jarek a strange feeling. It was not necessarily strictly a feeling of darkness—it was a mix of sadness, darkness, hopelessness, and clearly had much activity occurring from each side of the veil. He took a deep breath while he began to walk to the front door. Jarek did not know how his unexpected arrival would be welcomed, but he was anxious to discover what was waiting for him at the O'Connell mansion.

Jarek followed the depression in the snow where the walkway was beginning to disappear under the falling snow. As he started up the path, a snow-dusted stray cat ran in front of him through the yard and rushed under the pine trees. The front of the home was adorned with garland all over and a wreath on each double door of the entrance. Jarek could faintly hear the sound of a piano playing. He paused on the front stoop, choosing not to ring the bell while the song was in progress. He thought to himself that it would be rude of him to interrupt such a lovely song.

As soon as the song concluded, Jarek began to reach for the bell to announce his presence. However, before he could pull the rope, the door suddenly opened. Standing in front of him was a woman dressed in a dark charcoal gray dress with a high collar. Her hair was dark but beginning to gray. The hair was pulled back tightly in a bun.

Jarek quickly took a step back out of surprise.

"Good evening, sir. May I help you?" she asked Jarek while looking at him with an expression of total inconvenience.

"Yes, ma'am," Jarek replied, still with a hint of being startled in his voice. He cleared his throat, "I am here . . . Ah, I have been sent to research some of the happenings here at the home."

The woman continued to stare at Jarek, narrowing her eyes. Jarek begin to realize the home likely has had many visitors recently. People conducting the investigation into the murder and people giving condolences to the family.

"Well, sir, do you have a name that I can share with Mr. O'Connell so he may know who is currently on his property?" she asked with a stern tone.

"Ah . . . yes . . . Apologies, ma'am," he stuttered slightly. "My name is Jarek Videni. I'm from New York City."

"Very well, I shall inform him you are here . . ."

"Thank you so much," Jarek responded quickly.

"You may follow me into the parlor to come out of the cold." She gestured for him to enter the home. "The parlor is through this door," she said as she proceeded to guide him through the elegant foyer, through a large archway into a room with several couches and chairs, a fireplace, and a piano. She gestured toward one of the chairs. "You may sit here while you wait for Mr. O'Connell."

"Thank you," Jarek replied, feeling awkward as he was debating to remove his coat and such, or if that would be overstepping his welcome.

Jarek simply set his small suitcase and satchel down and sat on the chair as the woman turned and walked out of the room. He looked around the room, impressed by the woodwork, the ornamental rug, and the various paintings and figurines. He saw a beautifully framed map of the entire city of Saint Paul.

Jarek noticed the piano sitting near the window. He wondered to himself if it was the woman who greeted him at the door who had been playing so beautifully just a moment ago. As he stared at the piano, the fine hairs on his neck and arms begins to stand, and he began to feel a hint of tingle throughout his entire body. Jarek knew he was currently being watched. Before he could think much about it, he could hear multiple sets of feet approaching the parlor. He quickly sat up straight in his chair.

"Good evening, Mr. Videni!" said a man turning the corner into the parlor. The man was well-dressed, looked to only be about forty years old, and had a very friendly face. "Welcome to our home," he said while beginning to stretch out his arm to shake Jarek's hand.

Jarek stood from the chair, stretched out his arm in return, and shook his hand. "Please, sir, call me Jarek. Good to meet you, Mr. O'Connell. You have a beautiful home here."

"Thank you, thank you. And you may call me Martin," he replied to Jarek. "Your arrival is a surprise, as we didn't know any more investigators were to arrive prior to the Christmas holiday. But do not misinterpret me; I am very grateful for any assistance you are able to provide."

Jarek noticed the woman who let him in was continuing to stand by the archway, almost to insinuate she was ready for Jarek to gather his belongings so she could show him out the door.

"Well, Martin, I certainly would not want to impose on you during the holiday. I can go find a hotel and return after Christmas if that is more convenient for you?"

"Oh, certainly not! I am not going to send you away after such a long trip. I enjoy having another person around the house anyway, and we certainly have the room to host a guest." He turned and looked at the woman in the archway. "Rose, please ready one of the guest rooms for Mr. Videni, and ensure he has a place at the dinner table for this evening."

"Yes, sir," she replied, before turning and walking away.

"Again, sir … I mean, Martin, I am sorry if this is any inconvenience to you during this time."

"Oh, nonsense, we had so many people here during those first initial weeks after Sarah's death that it was becoming an annoyance, frankly. However, then it seemed so quick to disappear from the minds of the authorities. Like her death suddenly didn't matter simply because they could not find any answers."

"I'm very sorry to hear that. I am sure that has to be frustrating. Though I do not know what assistance I can provide you and your family yet, I will do everything within my power that I can to help bring some peace and closure."

"Well, that is all I can ask for Jarek. I do truly mean that, and also if you need anything while you are here, please do not hesitate to ask myself or Rose."

"That was the woman that greeted me at the door, correct?" Jarek asked.

"Yes," Martin said while taking a slight pause. "Rose can give the impression of . . . well . . . not welcoming. Nevertheless, that is because she is protective of our family and home. Especially since the death of Sarah. She has let that personality trait exacerbate lately."

"Understandably so. I hope my tone did not sound too judgmental of her."

"No, no, not at all. I was simply giving an explanation to you, for if she ever does present herself as too brash. She has been part of our family for nearly thirty years. She found employment with us when I was just a boy. She was not from here and was with child out of wedlock, but my mother took pity on her and offered employment. After I became successful and built this house, I knew I needed her assistance in helping to manage the staff and helping Sarah with raising our daughter Annie."

"That is very admirable, and I am sure she is quite grateful for your family."

"Oh yes! She hesitated to come here initially, but my parents both passed away prior to this house being completed, so once it was finished, she moved right in. She helped with hiring the staff and took immediate ownership of the home and her duties as governess."

Suddenly, the grandfather clock in the foyer began to sound.

"Well, it is seven thirty p.m. already. It's time for dinner."

"Thank you, but I already had an early dinner at the train depot."

"Nonsense, you must still join us. Besides, you have yet to meet my daughter, Annie," Martin said as he stood and started to turn and walk out of the parlor.

Jarek gathered up his belongings, and Martin led him back through the foyer. Jarek noted a grand double staircase with a double door under the center where they met. The ornate architecture impressed him. Martin shared about the construction process as the two men continued walking toward the dining room. The eyes Jarek felt on him in the parlor continued to watch him throughout the journey through the foyer.

Martin was finishing talking about the ins and outs of managing such a large construction crew when, suddenly, Jarek noticed a shadow entity peering from behind the grandfather clock. The hair on his neck stood up from being somewhat startled, combined with a chill that swept through the room simultaneously. Jarek returned his gaze back to Martin walking, then back toward the grandfather clock. The entity was gone.

Martin walked through the tall doorway into the dining room. Inside, Jarek saw more of the beautiful paintings, elaborate drapes on the windows, a beautiful marble fireplace, and a table designed to seat twelve people. It was the largest dining room that Jarek had ever stepped foot in.

"Please, Jarek, have a seat here," Martin said while pulling a chair out next to the head of the table. "Annie should be down here at any moment."

"I'm here, Father," said a young woman walking briskly through the doorway into the dining room. "I apologize, I was upstairs reading," she said as Martin began to pull a chair on the far side of the table out for her to sit at. However, she reached past him and pulled the plate setting one place further away from his chair.

"Annie, this is Jarek," Martin said as the young woman continued to establish herself at her self-assigned seat. Martin seemed to basically ignore her actions, as if this were a common occurrence. "He is here to help with the ongoing investigation."

"Hopefully he has better luck than the rest of the 'officials' here in this city," Annie blurted out, sounding annoyed. She just looked directly at her place setting and seemed to refuse to make any eye contact with Martin or Jarek.

"You'll have to excuse my daughter. She has had a hard time dealing with the death of Sarah," Martin said, looking up at Jarek with sadness in his eyes. "Rightfully so, of course," he quickly said, as not to offend Annie.

"Of course," Jarek agreed sympathetically.

Jarek could feel tension between the father and daughter. He knew a family going through a tragedy such as this was likely to bring out either the best or the worst in people. He set his satchel and suitcase down near the doorway and then took his seat at the table near Martin, kitty-corner from Annie. After a few moments of silence, dinner began to be served to them. All three ate in almost total silence, with no talking. Jarek continued to feel the tension while only hearing the clanking of the silverware on the plates. It seemed like time stood still from the lack of any talking. He noticed that everyone was nearly finished with their food, so he decided to attempt to relieve the thick atmosphere of the room.

"This pork loin is delightful. Thank you so much for the meal."

"Oh, it is our pleasure. Like I said earlier, we have had so many people in and out of this house over the past several weeks . . . then suddenly nothing. So it is good to have a new person coming here to bring a new perspective and energy to the home."

Martin continued talking about the many people from all over the Midwest that had come into their home to help investigate the situation. Jarek could see Annie avoiding the conversation. He assumed she was so tired of the whole situation, so this was likely her coping mechanism. Jarek was facing Martin so as to not be rude while he was talking, but he was watching Annie in his peripheral vision.

Jarek could tell that Annie was greatly struggling in this situation. *Dealing with the loss of a parent at such a young age must be unbearable*, he acknowledged to himself. Jarek never knew his father, as his mother had given birth to him out of wedlock and rarely talked about his father. His mother and grandmother raised him. It is hard to lose anyone, but it is less likely as hard to lose someone who is further along in years than to lose a mother so young. As he continued to half-listen to Martin, he was thinking about Annie's handling of the death of her mother: *She has likely lost the most important person in her life, without any answers or closures.* Jarek felt much empathy for the girl. He knew he needed to help this family.

Jarek began getting deeper and deeper in thought, when suddenly he could see a manifestation beginning nearly right over the chair between Martin and Annie. It began as a small flicker, slowly growing into a full sphere. He knew no one else could see this, so he tried not to give any reaction to it. This manifestation was an occurrence that he had never experienced. He had seen orbs before in their full beauty, however, never in the presence of others. In his experience and understanding, an orb was a human spirit that technically has found peace and crossed over to the great beyond. These spirits' energies have passed back to this side of the veil typically because they were searching for guidance or were in need of some help. Immediattely, Jarek thought to himself that this could be Sarah attempting to reach out, but he could not channel his own energies toward the orb to attempt to gain an understanding. The orb simply hovered with a slight dance of elegance between the two individuals who were both clearly struggling emotionally.

"Well, is anyone in the mood for a bit of dessert?" Martin asked in a manner to clearly change the subject.

Jarek could tell Martin wanted to talk more about the ongoing investigations as his way of handling the situation. Likely, the man's coping mechanism was to continue to hold out hope. By continuing to talk about Sarah, she continued to stay alive in his eyes. However,

Annie clearly was totally lost in her thoughts and angry over the death of Sarah.

"Otherwise, we can retire to the parlor, or I suppose you wouldn't mind a tour of the house and to settle into your room, Jarek?"

"I would really like that. It would be greatly appreciated," Jarek said as he watched the orb disappear like a mist. "I . . . I would definitely like to freshen myself up quickly," he said as he fully transitioned his attention back to Martin.

"Excellent! Rose, please come into the dining room and show Mr. Videni to his room so he may settle in," Martin said loudly.

Rose came into the room immediately, as if she had been waiting by the doorway for that very request.

"Certainly, Mr. O'Connell," Rose said in the same monotone stoic manner Jarek witnessed earlier. "Mr. Videni, please follow me," she said as she turned back toward the foyer.

"Thank you," Jarek said. "Please excuse me, Martin, Miss O'Connell. I will meet you in the parlor in thirty minutes for the tour of the home," he said as he stood from his seat. He walked to the door, reclaiming his belongings to bring to his room. "After you, Ms. . . . ?" Jarek said in an inquiring manner.

"Smith. My name is Rose Smith, Mr. Videni. Please follow me."

"Thank you, Ms. Smith," Jarek responded quickly.

Rose had a cold manner about her. Yet Jarek felt an underlying comfort with her. He could tell she cared deeply for this home and family. She likely exhibited this coldness to all new people in the home. Rose led Jarek into the foyer and up the staircase.

"I am sure Mr. O'Connell will give you a tour of the home in great detail, so I won't show you much except your quarters. The second floor consists of the family's bedrooms, the primary guest bedroom, and the library," Rose stated as they got to the top of the stairs on the platform for the second floor. "The third floor is more guest quarters, where I stay. There is space for any of the workers who are unable to make it home when inclement weather hits. The house may feel big, but I assure you that you will find it well planned out."

She opened the very first door on the left.

"This is the largest of the guest rooms in the house. You will find the fireplace stays well-lit with no drafts. There is a small closet to keep your belongings, along with direct access to a private bath. Mr. O'Connell insisted on having electricity and plumbing throughout the house when it was built. All the latest conveniences."

"This will do wonderfully, Ms. Smith. I cannot thank you enough," Jarek said genuinely.

"You're welcome, Mr. Videni. If you should need anything at all, there is a pull rope here and a speaking tube to ring the worker's area downstairs in the kitchen. Someone will respond through the speaking tube or come to your door directly if they hear the bell ringing."

"Thank you again. I better quickly freshen up and head downstairs to the parlor."

Rose turned and left the room, closing the door behind her. Jarek walked further into the room, admiring the large bed to his right, the closet doors across to his left, and the door to the private bathroom. Straight ahead was a large window, and next to it on the left, a fireplace. A small table sat near the window with a chair, and a very comfortable-looking armchair sat facing the fireplace.

Jarek felt as though this room was too extravagant. Nevertheless, he was going to take full advantage. After setting his belongings on the bed, Jarek proceeded into the bathroom to wash his face before going downstairs to the parlor. Once he finished swishing water in his mouth, he splashed some water on his face. As he was patting his face dry, a chill swept through the room.

Jarek felt an entity, or entities, passing through the room. A shadow sped past behind him. He could swear he heard whispering out in his room. Jarek went to identify where the talking was coming from. The energy of several spirits hit him at once. They seemed to swirl about in the room when he walked in. Energies seemed to be coming from the fireplace, the closet, and the speaking tube near the door.

The voices were not at a volume any average person could decipher. Jarek had heard spirits whisper many times. Sometimes he could understand them, and other times it seemed as if they spoke in another language. Oftentimes they spoke at a decibel that only they could communicate in. The entity or entities in his room currently were whispering in the decibel only they could understand. Jarek tried to focus on the whispers to begin to understand what was being said when they suddenly stopped and were gone. Whatever just came into the room was there and gone in a manner of minutes.

Jarek had never felt such strong energy in such a short amount of time. For entities to be simply passing through, it hit Jarek hard. This house truly had something occurring. Something that he must find out in order to discover the answers to Sarah's death.

Jarek knew he needed to get downstairs to the parlor to meet Martin for the full tour of the home, so he began to cross the room. As he walked past the bed, his satchel that he had set there fell off the edge and landed on the floor. He turned around and saw that one of the letters he received had spilled out onto the floor. Jarek bent down, picked up the satchel, and returned it to the bed. He then grabbed the letter off the floor. It was the first letter he had received. He knew that he was supposed to read it again. He carefully pulled the letter from its envelope, unfolding it gently. Clearly worn-out, Jarek had read it many times since receiving it about four weeks prior.

Dear Mr. Videni,

We have never met, but I know you through commonalities. I did not know who else to turn to at this time. I can't explain much, and that is the problem. I live in a home that is in dire need of your help. There was a great tragedy in this home on August 16th. There was a gruesome murder in this house. I do not know by whom or by what. Nobody does.

The investigation is still ongoing. Normally, I would have faith in the local authority; however, a few days ago, I began to witness events in this house that I cannot explain. I believe that the victim of the murder is trying to reach out to me. I deeply believe that this death was not a random act, or even an earthly act. Something dark has entered this home. I can hear it, I can smell it, and I can feel it. Please, Mr. Videni, come to the residence of Mr. Martin O'Connell in Saint Paul, Minnesota. Your gifts can help rid this home of darkness and perhaps help her find peace.

—I anxiously await your arrival

Jarek slowly reread the letter, hoping for more clues. Nothing came to mind. He gently folded the letter back up and placed it in the envelope. He then tucked it into his satchel once again. Jarek scanned his room one more time before turning around and exiting the room to meet Martin in the parlor.

CHAPTER 3

THE LIBRARY

December 20, 1924, 9:17 p.m.

The atmosphere in the parlor was calm and quiet as Jarek stepped foot into the room. Martin sat in the same chair Jarek had sat in earlier when he had first arrived. Martin sat there reading the newspaper and smoking a pipe.

"Ah, there you are! Did Rose get you settled into your room upstairs?" he asked Jarek in an upbeat tone.

"Oh, yes! The room is far too kind. Very spacious and . . . uh . . . seems to have lots to offer," Jarek responded while trying not to sound disturbed by the odd event he had just experienced a few moments ago in the bedroom. "I am sure I'll have a very comfortable stay."

"Excellent. Again, thank you for coming here during this time. I can't remember, which official here in Saint Paul reached out to you to assist with solving this case?"

"Actually, I don't think I told you," Jarek answered with a little hesitation, while he walked over and sat in a chair near where Martin was sitting. "I honestly don't know who reached out to me. I received a letter with concerns about the case, and the person believed that with . . . Well, with my skill set, that I would be able to assist you."

Martin took a deep breath.

"Fascinating . . . And the letter was unsigned by the person requesting your presence?"

"Yes, sir," Jarek responded reluctantly.

Martin's demeanor changed. He sat straight up, tightening up, and appearing to be less friendly to Jarek. "Interesting . . ." Martin trailed off, taking another deep breath. "Well, OK, I should show you around the house," he stated, suddenly sounding perkier once again.

"Yes, that would be perfect, Martin," Jarek responded, happily changing the subject back to the home itself and away from the letters.

They both stood up simultaneously from their chairs, adjusting their clothing, ready to begin the tour of the home.

"Well, obviously this room is the parlor. This is one of my favorite rooms in the home. Since this is one of the first impressions someone has when coming here, I wanted it to leave a lasting impression," Martin said with a hint of boastfulness in his tone.

"This room definitely meets that objective. I know I was certainly taken aback when I walked in. The high ceilings, the woodwork, the artwork, and that beautiful piano. It made me rub my peepers in disbelief of its beauty," Jarek said, being honest with Martin on the grandness of the room. "I have always wished that I had continued to learn how to play the piano. Would be wonderful to play on one this beautiful."

"Yes, this was brought in from Chicago. Sarah had fallen in love with it on a trip we took there while the house was being built. Oh, how she loved to play it. Sadly, it doesn't get used anymore," he stated in a quiet and solemn manner.

Jarek remembered the music he could hear when he had first arrived on the front steps of the house. *Was I imagining it all?* Jarek thought to himself with bewilderment. "Does no one else play in the household?" he asked, slightly confused.

"Sadly, no. No one in the home plays anymore. Sarah had wanted Annie to learn, but she hated it. Annie was more consumed by her studies and reading, and thought herself too busy to learn something as trivial as the piano," Martin said, almost with a small grin, as he was likely comparing the stark differences between Sarah and Annie in his mind. "Thankfully, Sarah was able to help teach . . ." He paused. "She taught some of the staff over the years." He sighed slightly. "I sure wouldn't mind hearing those keys being played again."

Still befuddled by knowing he heard it played just earlier that evening, Jarek thought it best to change the subject. "So, shall we continue? I am anxious to see the whole place."

"Yes, yes of course."

Martin began to lead them from the parlor through the grand foyer again. While walking through the foyer, he continued to explain the process of the planning and construction of the house. Jarek was genuinely interested in the information he was receiving from Martin; however, he continued to split his attention between listening to Martin and keeping tuned into the home and the strange energies within.

The two men moved on to the dining room briefly, since Jarek had already seen that room. They then moved quickly through the kitchen and servants' area beyond a doorway from the rear of the dining room. It was by far the largest kitchen Jarek had ever seen, with an area for the staff to relax a bit when able, and, just beyond that, an entry leading out to the back of the home. Jarek concluded that this door must lead to the carriage house and the path that wrapped around to the front of the house he had seen when first arriving to the O'Connell mansion.

There were three staff members in the kitchen just finishing cleaning up from the evening meal. They were gathering their belongings and were ready to go to their homes for the night. Rose was standing in the kitchen ensuring everything was accomplished to her standards.

"Ms. Smith, it's nearly ten p.m. May we leave for the evening?" one of them asked her, just quietly enough as to not be rude while Martin was continuing to talk to Jarek about the fine details of designing and building a kitchen of this magnitude.

"Yes, of course," Rose responded quietly. "Be safe in this weather," she said to them as the two women and the young man finished bundling up in their coats and hats.

They left quietly out the back entry.

"See you tomorrow, ma'am," the man said to Rose as the door latched behind them.

"Rose, would you like to accompany us on the remaining tour of the home before retiring for the evening?" Martin asked, noticing the staff had just left.

"I have a few more items I wanted to finish up tonight before retiring. Is it all right if I complete those tasks and then join you and Mr. Videni in a bit?"

"Yes, of course, Rose. We are going to move on to the ballroom, and then I'll quickly show Jarek the third floor before finishing on the second floor."

"Of course, sir. Thank you," Rose said as she walked out of the room.

She carried herself with poise, yet anytime she walked near Jarek, he noticed she would look away. She gave the continued impression of annoyance with him. He felt she clearly made a point as to not interact directly with him. Jarek continued to believe that this annoyance was due to Sarah's death. The constant interruptions of daily life by the continued investigation and likely her internalized need to govern this home like a well-oiled machine in order to ensure Martin and Annie had no inconveniences in their lives. The deeper he thought about that mindset, the more Jarek admired her dedication to the home and family during these times ... even if he never did feel as welcomed into this home by her the same way Martin has welcomed him.

"As you can tell, I love for people to visit, for people to feel our hospitality, and to ensure that they have fun while here. So, Jarek, the last room to see on this floor is my absolute favorite: the ballroom."

Martin put his arm around Jarek, turning him toward the door in the kitchen that led directly into the ballroom. He turned the knob of the door and pulled it inward, revealing the majestic room that Martin was so proud of and that often astounded people. The wood flooring color and shine were so regal, laid in a beautiful Art Deco pattern. The massive windows stood at least fifteen feet tall, allowing anyone occupying the room to see outside to the evergreen trees and the night sky beyond. Off to the side of the windows, tucked into the corner, sat an ornate harpsichord.

The walls were covered in beautiful wainscoting. The portions that were not wood were covered in majestic foil paper of deep blue and gold coloring. The decorative wall sconces were made of brass, with small crystals hanging from them and accompanying electric bulbs.

However, even though everything was worth staring at, what stood out the most in this glamorous room was clearly the chandelier hanging down directly in the middle of the room. It was nearly eight feet wide and six feet tall. It was made of hundreds if not thousands of crystals. It was fully electric, so it illuminated the entire room. A person could get lost looking at its depth, sparkle, and beauty.

Jarek felt that this room alone was fancier than any room he had ever stepped foot in. After a few moments, taking everything in visually, Jarek broke the silence.

"Well, Martin, I must say this room is one of the most visually appealing things my eyes have ever seen."

"Thank you. I know it is too extravagant, but I wanted a place to host parties and a place for people to feel like they were really experiencing something special."

"You have definitely met that objective."

Jarek honestly felt special standing in this room. He felt as if he were a guest at a royal palace in Europe. "I imagine every person who steps foot in here feels that way. Martin, you must throw some amazing parties here."

Martin stared at the room, taking it all in as if it were his first time seeing it, too. "We certainly have over the years. Obviously, we have not had any lately, but that is going to change soon. I have decided to continue with our plans to host a Christmas Eve event. Despite Rose objecting and Annie being too immersed in her studies to even talk to me lately, I feel it is the best for our friends and this house to welcome people once again and bring life back into it."

"I think that is a very admirable approach, and I am sure it will be greatly appreciated by your friends."

"Well, I expect you to still be here, so I insist on your attendance!" Martin's demeanor became somewhat solemn. "You see, Jarek, I wasn't born into money. My family was never poor, mind you, but we were not wealthy. My father started the printing factory when I was a teenager, and we made it the success it is today. I spent my summers working at the logging mill several miles east of here . . ." Martin trailed off and suddenly seemed lost, deep within his own thoughts. He was looking directly at Jarek yet seemed to be almost looking through him.

"Martin?" Jarek asked, with no immediate response. "Mr. O'Connell, is everything all right?"

Martin slowly seemed to focus back on Jarek. "Ah, yes . . . sorry about that. Shall we continue with the tour? It is getting late."

"Yes, please," he responded, while staring at Martin.

As Martin walked past Jarek to continue out the main doors of the ballroom into the foyer, his eyes remained looking directly forward, where Martin had been standing. A slight rancid smell hit Jarek's nostrils. He focused his eyes on the dimly lit corner of the room near the harpsicord. As he reached up to rub his nose, a shadow jolted from the corner directly at Jarek. Right as he began to flinch, the figure vanished like a mist. Jarek could not make out any definitive features of the entity, but by the energy and smell that came from it, he knew inside that it was an inhuman spirit.

Jarek gathered his thoughts quickly and hustled out of the room to catch up with Martin to finish the tour. His blood was still pumping, and the tiny hairs on his body were still standing fully erect from the jolt of energy. He passed through the main double doors from the ballroom back into the foyer. He noticed Martin already halfway up the staircase, so he hustled up the stairs.

"I thought I lost you back there. Just admiring the room some more?"

"Yes, sir, sorry. It just has . . . a lot to look at," Jarek responded.

"Oh, quite all right!" Martin said as he turned to continue walking up the stairs. "Oh, Rose. Just in time."

Jarek saw Rose on the landing of the second floor looking down on them.

"Rose, would you be willing to finish showing our guest the rest of the house? I am suddenly feeling very tired."

Jarek looked at Martin a bit puzzled, and then he looked up at Rose. She was looking right at Jarek as she responded to Martin.

"Certainly, sir," she said while giving her head a single nod. "Won't you follow me please, Mr. Videni?"

"Thank you, Rose," Martin said as he continued up the stairs, walking right past Rose and venturing down the second-floor hallway to his room.

"Thank you, Ms. Smith. I do appreciate it," Jarek said as he walked up to the second-floor landing to stand by Rose.

"Of course Mr. Videni," she replied in her usual monotone levels she had used with him thus far. "Follow me, please." She turned to continue walking up the staircase to the third floor, followed by Jarek in tow, but she turned and paused. "I must admit, sir, the third floor only consists of additional guest rooms and my own room. I know Mr. O'Connell likes to show everything during a tour, but if you don't mind, seeing the time is nearly eleven p.m. and you have . . . have had a long day, may we skip the third floor and just finish the tour here on the second?"

"Of course. I was honestly thinking the same thing," he replied.

Though Jarek was enjoying seeing the entire house, he was beginning to feel exhausted, and he wanted to think about the events that had taken place here tonight thus far.

Rose began to walk down the hallway.

"This first door on the right is the room of Miss Annie. You can find her most days spending time between her room and the library lately," she said with a slight sadness to her voice. "As you know, this door on the left is your room."

They both continued to walk down the hallway about another twenty feet or so. Jarek continued to be in awe over the sheer magnitude of this house.

"This door leads to Mr. O'Connell's bedroom," Rose said while gesturing to the second door on the right.

They both took a slight pause, as they could hear music playing very quietly on a phonograph. Martin was likely listening to some music while he was getting ready for bed.

"And finally, this door is to the library," Rose said as she opened the door across from the master bedroom.

The door she opened led into a beautiful library with ceilings two stories high. Two full levels of bookcases and a loft circled almost the entire room, allowing any person to reach each shelf. One corner had a beautiful desk, another a magnificent fireplace, another a spiral staircase going up to the loft, and another a reading nook. There were several chairs and a sofa arranged perfectly in the room, and just enough windows to allow for natural light during the day, but not to the greatness of the massive windows in the ballroom.

"This room is one of the family's favorites," Rose stated. "It still is used by Annie often, as she has recently become so immersed in studying and wanting to learn everything there is, it seems. Mrs. O'Connell also used this room extensively before her passing."

Rose halted her speech. Jarek knew immediately why she was pausing and becoming lost in her thoughts.

"This is the room where it happened, isn't it?" Jarek asked reluctantly.

"Yes. We found her remains right there at the base of the spiral staircase," she responded with a slight gesture. She clearly was feeling many emotions.

"Do you mind sharing with me what you know about the incident?"

"Yes, I can share what I witnessed, Mr. Videni."

"Of course. Feel free to only share what you wish. Any information would be of a great help."

"Have you researched anything about Mrs. O'Connell's death before coming here?"

"No, I'm afraid not, ma'am. This trip was made at the last minute, and I didn't seem to have adequate time to prepare."

"I . . . I understand," she responded.

Rose made her way to the green velvet sofa in the near corner. As she sat down, her demeanor once again was poised yet still cold.

"Well, it was August sixteenth, a Saturday. Mr. and Mrs. O'Connell had been at an event downtown. A rally for President Coolidge's campaign. Mr. and Mrs. O'Connell arrived back here to the home around four p.m. They were hosting a gathering planned for that evening here at the house for their friends. Oh, how they love having parties. Just as much as all their friends enjoy attending them. They would have one here at least once a month. Well, that evening was planned in the ballroom like usual; guests were to begin arriving after nine p.m. I had the staff prepare dinner early so the family would be able to eat their dinner and still have plenty of time to get ready before the guests arrived. After dinner, the family was upstairs in their rooms getting ready, I believe. I know there was a disagreement over something upstairs."

"A disagreement?"

"Yes, I'm sure it was about Annie not wanting to come down for the party. She found them to be boring and pointless recently. She would rather be in the library reading. It was hard on both Martin and Sarah, because Annie had always loved the parties, and guests expected to see Annie there. Nevertheless, Sarah would say it was Annie's choice to attend or not. Martin disagreed . . . It was Annie's duty to be there and to be a good hostess. They had argued about this prior to hosting some family members just a few weeks before that evening. Anyway, I could hear them a bit, as it does echo down through the speaking tubes in the walls from the rooms to the back entryway . . ." Rose continued to look coldly at Jarek as her voice trailed off. He believed she was alluding that she hears everything in this house. He did not know what to think of the mild threat.

"Were you able to understand . . . understand any of the conversation they were having?"

"No, not this particular one. I was more focused on the evening's guests, as they were beginning to arrive by then."

"I see. So did Mr. and Mrs. O'Connell come down once the guests began to arrive?"

"Yes. Mr. and Mrs. O'Connell entered the ballroom, probably around nine fifteen or nine thirty p.m. Annie entered closer to ten. However, they all looked happy and were having a wonderful evening."

"How many guests where there that evening?"

"We had nearly fifty guests . . . most of which were friends of Mr. O'Connell. Fellow businessmen from the city and such. On nights like this, there seems to be plenty of . . ." Rose trailed off once more but this time with a slight hint of embarrassment. "Well, plenty of drinks seem to go around. You see, Mr. Videni, being prominent members of the city, the O'Connell family get to enjoy a bit of clemency when it comes to the drink. To which their guests are all well aware and take full advantage. The Prohibition be damned, in their mind."

"Oh, I understand. I have witnessed it in New York City many times. Though us more common folk have to find our resources elsewhere," he responded with a slight grin.

Jarek always enjoyed a sip of giggle water or brandy when he had the chance. He wasn't going to lie about that to anyone, because he did not agree with the Prohibition and believed, as a consenting adult, he had a right to enjoy.

"Well, I believe some guests began to leave at about midnight. I know Annie went to retire for the evening at about twelve thirty in the night. The rest of the guests left shortly after one, and Mr. and Mrs. O'Connell went upstairs for the evening shortly after. The staff left as soon as everything was cleaned up, and I went to my room at about two thirty. I decided to read a bit before bed to relax before going to sleep. Well, I must have nodded off. Shortly after three in the morning, I jolted from my chair, throwing my book halfway across my room."

"What awoke you?"

"I believe it must have been a sort of scream or something that echoed through the halls. I honestly do not remember. I just remember jolting up knowing something wasn't right. So I made my way down to the second floor. I opened Annie's door and saw her sound asleep in her bed. I moved down to the master bedroom. I knocked on the door gently. There was no response, so as I was reaching for the doorknob, just to peek and ensure they were fine, the door opened, and there stood Mr. O'Connell. He clearly had just woken up, too. He did not even have his robe on. He asked if I knew where Sarah was, as she was not in bed. Martin thought she maybe had gotten sick from too many drinks, but he said she was not in their lavatory either. I turned and opened the door into the library."

Rose stopped talking. She began to show some emotion, as her cheeks grew flush and her eyes a bit watery. A break from her typical stoic face.

"It's all right, Ms. Smith. Take your time."

She took a breath. "I opened the door into the library. A few of the lamps were on in the room. I could see Mrs. O'Connell's body lying halfway on the stairs there"—Rose gestured toward the stairs in the corner again—"and halfway on the floor. She looked as if she had maybe fallen or had passed out. Mr. O'Connell ran toward her and I followed closely behind. As we got closer, it was easy to see it was something much . . . something much worse."

Rose paused for a moment. Jarek did not want to intrude on her thoughts while she was remembering this terrible event.

"It was so much worse. There was so much blood on the floor. Her throat . . . it had been cut completely across, and there was so much blood on her chest. Mr. O'Connell scooped her body up in his arms. I will never forget the horrible screams that came from him. I could hear him as I ran out of the library and down the stairs to telephone the police. I remember running by Annie, and I told her not to go in the library. When I came back from telephoning the police, Mr. O'Connell was sitting on the floor, weeping. Annie stood near here, where we are seated now. I believe she was in a complete state of shock. The police came shortly after. The rest of the evening and the days that followed are honestly a blur."

"I can't even begin to imagine that experience and those feelings. The family is fortunate to have you here, Ms. Smith."

Rose continued to look blank in the face, ignoring what Jarek had just said to her. She quickly brushed away a tear that began to roll down her cheek.

"I'm sorry, but I think I must retire for the evening. It is getting very late."

"Yes, I agree. I need to get some rest as well. Thank you, Ms. Smith, for sharing that. I know it can't be easy for you," Jarek responded.

They both stood from the sofa and began to walk out of the room. As soon as they reached the doorway, Rose turned and looked back at where Sarah's body had been discovered.

"The coroner said she had almost thirty stab wounds in her chest. And her"—she took a long pause, breathing deep—"her heart was . . . was completely removed."

"Her heart had been removed?"

"Yes," she answered as she gently shut the door to the library and began to walk down the hallway toward the stairs, with Jarek shortly behind her.

"Why on earth . . . Why on earth would someone rip a heart from someone's chest and discard it like rubbish?" Jarek said as he opened the door to his bedroom.

He immediately realized he said that statement aloud. Jarek looked at Rose. She was rigid once again.

"You don't understand, Mr. Videni," Rose said as she slowly turned back and looked directly at Jarek. "The killer not only took the heart from Sarah's chest; they took it with them. It was nowhere to be found."

CHAPTER 4

THE SIXTH CARD

December 21, 1924, 12:52 a.m.

Jarek's eyes opened wide as if startled by a loud noise. He continued to lie still on the bed. Something felt wrong. He could feel that he was not alone in the large bedroom. As he shifted his eyes toward the foot of the bed, he could see a shadow rush through the room. Then it was gone in the blink of an eye. It must have been just another traveling spirit passing through that awoke him, Jarek thought to himself.

Jarek continued to lie there thinking about the interactions he had throughout the day, getting to know the family, and hearing Rose's story of finding Sarah's body. He continued to be outright confused about the situation. Jarek knew there was something peculiar and wrong with the circumstances in this house. He continued to be at a total loss.

As Jarek continued his examination of the situation in his mind, he got a chill. The hairs on his arms and neck began to prickle. He knew it was not just the passing shadow that awoke him. He was still not alone in the room.

"Jaaarrek . . ."

A faint whisper broke the silence in the room.

Jarek's response to the voice was to become motionless.

"Jaaarrrek . . ." the voice spoke again.

Suddenly, Jarek could hear the faint sound of breathing. Slow deep breaths, as if someone was right next to him in the bed.

Jarek proceeded to tilt his head slightly in order to expand his vision of the room. He turned his head to the side, in the direction he believed the breathing was coming from. He began holding his breath in anticipation of a person or an entity being next to him. Jarek thought to himself that perhaps it was the entity from the ballroom earlier that night.

Nothing. Nothing was lying in the bed next to him. Jarek relaxed a bit, letting out a sigh of relief. As his eyes continued to adjust to the room, his vision was becoming clearer. Suddenly he could see that he was indeed not alone in the bedroom.

A figure stood directly in the corner of the room. It was a shadowy human-shaped figure. Jarek continued to watch the figure, but it remained motionless. It simply stood there as if it had been watching Jarek sleep.

It was still too dark in the room for Jarek's eyes to make out refined details of the figure. He slowly leaned over in the bed toward the nightstand to turn on the electric lamp. In his mind, Jarek expected the figure to leap at him as he turned the lamp on. However, as he reached for the lamp, the figure continued to stand completely still.

Once the lamp illuminated the room, Jarek was taken aback by the figure. There in the corner stood Martin O'Connell. He was in only his boxer shorts, staring directly at Jarek. However, his eyes were clearly focused somewhere else and not fixated on Jarek specifically.

"Mr. O'Connell," Jarek said, with a slight shake of nervousness in his voice.

There was no response.

Jarek stood up from the bed and approached Martin. He reached his hand out and placed it on Martin's shoulder, shaking him slightly. "Martin?"

Martin continued to stare blankly, looking straight ahead and breathing deep. His eyes were blank and his pupils enlarged. Jarek soon realized Martin was sound asleep. He must have been sleepwalking and ended up in Jarek's room.

"Mr. O'Connell . . . Martin," said Jarek, unsure of what to do aside from waking him up.

Jarek jumped slightly as his bedroom door creaked open just a bit.

"Father?" asked Annie as she peered her head through the door.

She quickly noticed Jarek was awake, too.

"Oh, I am very sorry, Mr. Videni. I had gone to check on my father because I thought I had heard him sleepwalking again past my bedroom door."

"No need to apologize. He startled me, is all. Does he do this often?"

"He does. It seems to occur more often now . . . these days."

"I haven't been around a sleepwalker before."

"He doesn't typically remember doing it."

"Would you like some help escorting him back to his room?" Jarek asked.

"I can handle it, Mr. Videni, but thank you for offering," replied Annie.

She gently placed her arm around her father's shoulders and began to turn him slowly toward the doorway. As she turned him, he reached out with both arms and placed them directly on Jarek's shoulders. He looked directly into Jarek's eyes as if trying to read his thoughts, not saying a word.

"Father, we must get you back to your room" Annie said, seeming a bit worried about his behavior.

"Mr. O'Connell, you need to follow Annie back to your room and get back into bed," Jarek said in a calm yet firm voice.

"Always keep your inner eyes open—things are not always what they seem," he said directly to Jarek. He turned and began to follow Annie out of the room. However, once he was crossing the threshold, he turned and said, "And my name is Peter."

Jarek stood there very confused.

"He gets confused at times when he is sleepwalking," replied Annie. "It's of no concern." She escorted her father from the room and closed the door tightly behind them.

Jarek stood there for a moment trying to figure out what just transpired in the past few moments. He was not so much startled by the thought of Martin in his room from sleepwalking. Rather, Jarek was more startled from Martin calling himself Peter. In addition, Jarek was concerned that Martin must call himself Peter frequently, because Annie did not seem a bit surprised by Martin's words.

This was just another piece to the ever-growing puzzle that was occurring in the O'Connell mansion. Jarek's mind continued to shuffle through everything when he realized the whisper of his name earlier was not Martin's voice. Jarek started to walk toward the bed as a bead of sweat moved down his forehead. *Who could have been trying to talk to me?* Jarek questioned in his head.

Jarek was about to get back into the comfort of his bed, but as he was leaning in toward the bed, he could see his leather satchel sitting on the elaborate wingback chair near the fireplace. He could feel a pull inside that he should try to gain some insight and understanding on the situation. Jarek knew he needed some guidance to try and see a clearer picture here. Perhaps he would be able to gain some outside perspective on the death of Sarah O'Connell and discernment on who sent the correspondences asking him to come to Saint Paul, or at least just insight on the oddities of this household.

Jarek stoked the logs in the fireplace and added one more to help rewarm the room and provide some more light than just what the little electric lamp provided. He preferred natural light provided by flames instead of the light from electrical lamps anyway. There were several candles sitting on the mantel above the fire, so Jarek grabbed three of the larger pillar-style candles and placed them on the small table near the fireplace.

Jarek walked over and put on the undershirt he had placed on the back of the chair earlier before going to sleep. He reached into his satchel and began rummaging through a few of his belongings: candles, smudge sticks, the journal he kept to document his findings, and finally at the bottom, he retrieved his set of Tarot cards.

Jarek retrieved a starter stick from the mantel and lit it from the fire. He proceeded to light the candles on the table, then snuffed out the stick and placed it back on the mantel. He saw a beautiful mantel clock and noticed it was 1:28 a.m. already. As he began to take his seat in the chair, he could already begin to feel a strong presence, and he could feel other energies were beginning to manifest and willing to help him.

While contemplating which spread he was going to use, Jarek knew nearly instantly he should do a five-point spread with the major arcana cards only. This spread allows him to turn a card for each person he wanted to gain insight on. Martin, Annie, Rose, Sarah, and he would each make the five points of the star.

Jarek began to shuffle the cards in his hand while thinking about each person who appeared to be a piece in this bizarre puzzle. Once Jarek felt he placed an adequate amount of thought and energy into the cards, he began to pull cards and place them facedown to make the five points of the Tarot spread. After he laid the fifth card to make the bottom right point, he began to feel a strong presence in the room, possibly multiple ones. One presence particularly became a clear shadow moving past him in the room. It moved farther away from the chair Jarek was sitting in toward the bed. It appeared as though it was someone facing away from him while it drifted through the room. This entity came in so clear that Jarek began to focus on it more, which resulted in him nearly losing his grip on the deck of cards. As Jarek regained his grip on the cards, an additional card fell out and landed on the floor next to the chair. The shadow stopped moving away immediately when the card touched the floor. The shadow was about ten feet away, directly in front of the bed. It continued to keep its back toward Jarek.

Jarek's eyes shifted and began to gaze upon the Tarot spread, channeling his energy to gain insight on the individuals surrounding the situation. It did not have a delineation of which card was for each person, but Jarek hoped he would be able to delineate which cards represented each person once he began the reading.

Taking a deep breath, Jarek flipped over the first card to reveal The Fool. This bright image showed a young man standing on a cliff's edge over the ocean. He was carrying a bindle, indicating he was on a journey. He held a white rose beginning to bloom in his other hand. Jarek knew, in general, he could interpret this card to mean an exciting new beginning was coming or that the person this card related to was on the verge of making a big decision or a major self-discovery.

Without much effort, Jarek instantly felt that this card related to him and his current situation accurately. He had taken a major leap of faith in trusting that the letters he received would bring him a new challenge in his abilities and that he would be able to help a family in need. However, he also knew that though he already had experienced spiritual activity from entities from the other side of the veil, he needed to take a pause, remain open-minded, and absorb everything in his surroundings. By seeing The Fool, Jarek felt he had made the right decision to come here. He could learn much during this case.

Suddenly, there was motion in the room again. Jarek looked up from the card slowly. He could see the figure near the bed move and appear to now rest upon it. Jarek had a feeling of ease inside, as well as a tug of confusion on this entity.

Jarek turned the second card over, the second point of the pentagram. The Hierophant—inverted from Jarek's perspective. A grand or royal individual was depicted on the face of the card. They were seated on a thronelike chair with a pillar of stability on each side. When this card is revealed in a spread, it typically represented that the individual was for traditional rules and social norms; they were set in their lifestyle and spiritual ways. However, when the card was inverted, that meant a more traditional person might be breaking social norms.

Jarek felt this card referred to Martin, who might feel this way because he was currently in a situation in which he may need to let go of traditional beliefs in order to begin his own healing process. Jarek knew that this card signified that Martin was currently dealing with his battles. Additionally, when looking at the card, there were two people, backs turned, looking onward to The Hierophant. Jarek contemplated the significance of this for a while. He wondered if it meant two different people were looking to Martin for strength and guidance or if it meant that inside, Martin himself felt like he had two different paths he could take . . . he just needed guidance and time.

Jarek took a pause before turning the third card over. Then, while taking a deep breath, Jarek's hand turned the card to reveal The Hermit, an image of an old man cloaked in gray. He carried a lantern and held a staff. He stood on the tops of mountains, indicating reflection around him, yet he was looking downward. This looking down indicated inward reflection.

Jarek immediately associated this with Annie. He knew that The Hermit often represented someone who works best in solitude. An additional interpretation could mean that an individual needs to take the time to self-reflect in order to find solace. Jarek had heard several times now that since Sarah's passing, Annie had turned to reading and studying in a manner of dealing with the situation. However, Jarek believed that if The Hermit were inverted, it would have been more reflective of her. When inverted, the card would be insinuating that through reclusion and soul searching, someone could deal with a situation. That now would be the time to take the next step and move forward.

Jarek reflected back on dinnertime and how Annie had behaved. She clearly was consumed by the situation and did not know how else to deal with her mother's passing except by focusing solely on her reading and studies. Jarek became more concerned thinking about how Annie was spending the majority of her time in the very room that her mother was taken from her. Being consumed by grief could lead someone to become stagnant and to not fulfill a meaningful life. The more his mind sorted out the situation, The Hermit did not seem to fit Annie. *But who could it be?* Jarek pondered to himself. He decided to move on to the next card in hopes of identifying the person through process of elimination.

Jarek's hand took the fourth card, the fourth point of the pentagram, turning it over to reveal Temperance. The card depicted an angelic being maintaining balance and tranquility. The angel looked to be neither male nor female. It had one foot in the water, one on the ground next to a field. It had two cups, one in each hand, with water flowing between them. The reader was unable to determine which cup was pouring into the other, signifying perfect balance. This card had always been a favorite of Jarek's. It brought an internal calmness to him instantly. The person this card signified has found peace and contentment.

Jarek's brain began to scramble to see whom this could represent. Each person he had encountered in this house, including himself, was far from content. The more he thought, the clearer it became to him—Sarah. This women's life had been taken far too soon, and in a gruesome manner. However, she must have found peace. She had moved on from this place and had found balance in this life and next. This logic would give reason to why the orb at dinner never fully manifested into anything more and only lasted for a short while.

A slight chill ran over Jarek's arms, causing his hair to stand upright. Similar to the feeling as when the entities came through his room earlier in the evening. It wasn't as dark of a feeling though. Suddenly, he could tell the energy was coming from the entity across the room. The energy confirmed to Jarek that if Temperance represented Sarah, she had moved on from this place. *If she was gone, who was this sitting in the room with him now?* he began to wonder. Jarek's emotions became overwhelmed with a sadness and loneliness from this entity . . . This entity was someone new.

Jarek turned the fifth and final card of the pentagram, revealing The Magician inverted. The image of the Magician showed someone having everything aligned in life currently, being able to influence events and have great skill. The card showed the tools of the minor arcana suit at their disposal for use: the cup, sword, wand, and pentacles. However, the card was inverted. This implied that someone was using everything in their power to get what they wanted. Someone in this house was cunning and was using manipulation to give a persona of someone they are not. Jarek felt by turning this card over he now was unsure of how to read the cards previous as to who they might relate to.

Jarek began to contemplate deeply. His eyes focused on the flames of the three candles on the small table. As they flickered, he saw the shadow across the way appear to stand back up. It paused, looking like a statue standing in front of the bed. Instantaneously, it rushed across the room, through the table, and through Jarek's body. As the shadow touched Jarek, his entire body felt the vibrations of energy that the entity was secreting. Jarek's mind suddenly felt as if he lost all hope in life and was trapped, isolated, and silenced—yearning for anything more, but then suddenly, nothing; everything went black.

Ж

After what felt like a few moments, Jarek regained consciousness. He realized he must have passed out from the surge of energy that went through his body when the entity touched him. He had never felt that sensation before. A massive feeling of utter and total emptiness and hopelessness. Once his eyes began to refocus, Jarek could see that the candles had gone out, likely when the entity rushed through the room. The logs in the fireplace still had a small flame. Jarek stood and retrieved a few more logs from near the fireplace and placed them on the smoldering embers. They quickly ignited and provided additional light and heat to dampen the chill in the room. After stoking the fire, Jarek looked at the clock on the mantel: 3:30 a.m. exactly. He must have been out cold for nearly an hour or more.

Jarek turned to set aside the five Tarot cards he had read. He intended to revisit them in the morning after he had gotten some sleep. When he began to reach for the cards, Jarek realized they were all restructured perfectly in the pentagram spread he had done earlier, but there was a sixth card placed directly in the middle of the star turned facedown. The other cards were in a different order than when he had previously revealed them. Someone or something had organized the cards in a particular order. *And where did this sixth card come from?* Jarek wondered to himself. He looked down toward the foot of the chair. He remembered a card had fallen from the deck earlier, but there was no card lying on the floor anymore. The sixth card that fell from the deck was no accident. It was intended to be read by Jarek, and somehow it was on the table now directly in front of him.

Scanning the cards again, Jarek looked at them in the new order. First The Hermit, then The Hierophant, followed by Temperance. Fourth in order sat the card that was yet to be revealed to Jarek, with the fifth card being The Magician, and lastly, The Fool.

Jarek turned over the card. The Hanged Man met Jarek's eyes. His internal feeling right away was that this was the card intended for him. His brain began to rush, to be consumed by the need to dissect the situation even further. Then he took a deep breath and returned his focus on The Hanged Man. This card was telling him to be open to looking at things from a new perspective. To remain calm and to primarily remain observant. To him, it meant that he needed to not be aggressive in finding answers, that the answers would expose themselves in due time. He needed to take a pause and absorb the clues lying around him. A feeling of contentment swept over Jarek as he realized he needed to allow new ideas or thoughts on the situation to come to him.

Jarek looked at the spread once more. He was fourth in whatever the order or pattern that this entity wanted him to find. He took the six cards and kept them in the same sequence before placing them on top of the remaining deck. Jarek placed the deck back into his satchel and set it on the floor. He moved over toward his bed, removed his undershirt once again, and crawled into the bed, lying on his back. He pulled the quilt right up to his chin to stay warm as he began to doze off, thinking about the card he had just read.

Jarek's eyes grew heavy, his breathing getting shallower as his body began to transition into sleep. His brain began to quiet down and stop swirling about from his attempts at decoding the pattern of the cards. Right when he was about to completely fall asleep, he felt a rustle in the blankets near his feet. His mind was hoping that he was already asleep and beginning to dream, because it felt as if there was something actually in the bed with him. Then suddenly nothing.

The blankets began to rustle more. Something began to move upward toward his stomach from his feet. Jarek realized it was not just moving up toward him under the quilt, it was slithering. He began to shake and breathe heavier as nervousness ran through his whole body. Moving slowly, Jarek grabbed the quilt and began to roll it down in order to reveal what was truly in bed with him. He continued slowly rolling the quilt down further. Time felt as if it were standing still to Jarek. His breathing grew even heavier as he began to sweat profusely. The slow slithering thing reached his abdomen. It was closing in on his chest. With one quick flip of the quilt, Jarek threw the blanket down.

There, resting directly on Jarek's chest, sat a viper, staring right at him. The serpent brought its head up and hissed, looking like it was ready to strike. Jarek quickly brought his forearm up to block the impending attack. He suddenly felt the long fangs of the snake puncture his skin as a loud sharp hiss came from the serpent. Then nothing. He lowered his arm. Surely he had just been bitten, he thought to himself. His mind was still panicking as he opened his eyes. Nothing was there. No viper, no threat. Nothing was in his room with him at all.

Jarek's mind told him the viper had to have been a vivid dream. But it felt so real. He brought the covers back over his body, turned to his side, and closed his eyes, hoping for a few hours of rest.

CHAPTER 5

LEONA

December 21, 1924, 8:32 a.m.

After what seemed to be only a few minutes, Jarek opened his eyes slowly. He had to blink several times because they were dry from the combination of the winter air and the hint of smoke from the fireplace burning all night. He rolled over toward the side table to look at the small clock: 8:32 a.m. His eyes shifted to the windows. It looked very gray and gloomy outside. He could see large fluffy snowflakes falling from the sky.

Jarek still felt groggy, only having about five hours of sleep. However, once the morning fog cleared from his brain, he remembered what had occurred last night. A slight panic returned to him as he thought about what happened after conducting the Tarot reading and when the viper struck him.

Jarek had had these types of dreams and hallucinations before. However, what concerned him the most was that these dreams were usually in cases where more than just spirits needed to move on—or a restless poltergeist. These cases were typically associated with malevolent spirits or inhuman beings. He knew that ever since arriving here, there was something dark taking place, but now he knew it was something that was truly malicious and intent on trying to frighten Jarek away.

As a gust of wind howled over the window, Jarek got a slight shiver just thinking about the cold air. He pushed the quilt over and stood up out of bed to get ready for the day. He was about to go throw a few logs on the fire to warm the room up more but decided that he should just hurry through his morning regimen.

After freshening up in his bathroom, Jarek walked out to get dressed and then go downstairs. As he was nearly done dressing, another gust of wind hit the window, making another howling sound. He turned just in time to see the large snowflakes blowing in the wind, nearly making visibility beyond the window impossible. However, it quickly quieted down. Jarek walked to the door, and as he was opening it to walk downstairs, he noticed a small folded piece of paper on the table next to the door. It lay directly below the bell pull rope and the speaking tubes. He secured it in his hand as he continued out of his room. While walking and unfolding the paper, he saw Annie exiting her room as well. She was dressed in a stylish black drop waist dress, buckle shoes, and a creamy white cardigan to help shoo away the cool air.

"Good morning, Miss O'Connell," said Jarek.

"Good morning, Mr. Videni. I hope you rested well last night after my father went back to bed," she replied in a much friendlier manner than she had during his interactions with her last night at dinner and later in his room.

"Yes, I got a few good hours of sleep in. Thank you."

"Excellent! I am heading down to the kitchen to get a bite to eat if you'd like to join me."

"Thank you, that would be marvelous," Jarek answered.

"What do you have there?" Annie asked, noticing Jarek was holding the half-unfolded piece of paper.

"Oh, it is just a note I found lying there," Jarek replied, gesturing toward his door.

He kept its origins somewhat vague on purpose. He finished unfolding it to see if it was of any importance before saying anything more.

"Well, what does it say?" she asked in a genuinely curious-sounding manner.

Jarek looked at the note. "It says, 'Dr. Monroe—Rice Park,'" Jarek said in a tone of befuddlement. There were no other markings on the piece of paper.

"That's odd. Father must have dropped it. Well, shall we go find some food?" Annie said as she turned to head downstairs.

"Yes, that would be excellent. But, what do you mean, your father must have dropped it?" Jarek asked.

"Well, yes. Dr. Monroe is his personal doctor. He must have moved locations or something, so father probably wrote it down."

"Ah, yes, that makes sense. I will be sure to give it to him."

As they started to walk downstairs in hopes of finding breakfast, Annie looked at Jarek for a few moments. "I am sorry again for interrupting your sleep last night. I am sure that was all very inconvenient after your long travels to get here," she finally said while staring at him.

"Thank you, Miss O'Connell . . ."

"Oh, please, call me Annie," she said as she gently moved in and put her arm around his as they crossed the foyer and continued toward the kitchen.

"Thank you, Annie. It was just fine. I have had far worse interruptions in my sleep before."

"Oh, I am sure. Did you serve during the Great War? I am sure there were many nights just as awful."

"Yes, I was over in France. You are not wrong, Annie. Many, many terrible nights. However, I accept your apology still. It was no bother, and I am just glad we got your father back into his bed."

"Oh, certainly. Trust me, these past few months, it seems that at least once a week, I wake up to find him wandering about the house. Sometimes I am so tired that I just figure, 'Gosh, just let him wander. He isn't hurting anything,'" she said with a small giggle. "Yum, I can smell fried pork belly and toast," she said as she let go of Jarek's arm and moved swiftly into the dining room.

Jarek followed her closely in tow. As he walked into the dining room, he saw Rose just finishing straightening up the two place settings on the table. They were in the same spots as the settings were originally last night for dinner.

"Oh, thank you so much, Rose. I didn't mean to come down here so late, but I slept in after staying up reading again," Annie said as she moved to her place setting and sat down.

"Certainly, Miss Annie. We all seem to have had a late evening."

Rose shifted her stare directly at Jarek, almost to insinuate blame on Jarek arriving. On the other hand, did she know about Jarek's own late night in his room? He wondered.

"But that's all right. It is easy enough to keep the food warm and coffee hot in the morning," Rose continued.

"Well, thank you again," Annie said. "Has father left for work yet this morning, or is he spending the day here at the house?"

"Yes, he has already left for the print factory earlier this morning. I think he said this was going to be his last day working there until after Christmas."

"Oh, I see. Thank you," Annie replied.

Her tone seemed to change, almost sounding sad. Jarek was debating if it was sadness emerging from her knowing that Martin was gone already for the day or that Martin was going to be home for the next several days. After witnessing her interactions with Martin during dinner last night, he was leaning toward the latter option. She clearly had some form of animosity toward Martin.

"Certainly, Miss Annie," Rose said, looking at her with concern. "I am going to go out for my morning errands. Is there anything you need me to pick up for you, Miss Annie?"

"Oh, no thank you. My dress won't be ready for pickup until tomorrow, after the final fitting," Annie replied.

Rose blinked, shifting her stare to Jarek once again. "Anything for you, Mr. Videni?"

"No, thank you, Ms. Smith," Jarek replied with a gentle smile to show appreciation and hopefully give her the realization he was not a threat.

"All right. I will return in several hours."

Rose turned and walked toward the kitchen doorway, stopping before stepping into the kitchen and turned back toward Annie and Jarek.

"Oh, and Miss Annie, we are having Beef Wellington this evening for dinner," Rose said with a smile and a wink.

"Oh, berries!" Annie exclaimed excitedly.

"I take it you enjoy Beef Wellington?" Jarek asked her with a big grin.

She responded with a smile, shaking her head yes.

"Me, too," he said, smiling as he began to dig into his breakfast.

Several minutes passed as they each ate their food, drank their coffee, and perused sections of the local daily newspaper, *The Saint Paul Dispatch*. Jarek felt completely at ease around Annie. She was a very pleasant girl, polite, and clearly had passion and drive.

"So, your father and Ms. Smith have told me that you have formed a strong habit of reading and studying lately," Jarek said in an inquisitive manner.

"Yes," was all Annie initially replied with.

Jarek turned his focus back toward the newspaper. He wanted to remain sensitive and did not want to prod too deeply.

"Sorry. I did not mean to be rude, Mr. Videni. It is just difficult sometimes. I do genuinely enjoy reading and learning things. But my father seems to think it is only my coping mechanism to this terrible year."

"No, I understand. When you are asked about your hobby, you feel like someone is truly asking about how you are handling your mother's passing?"

"Yes, exactly. I meant no offense. I enjoy not just novels; any studies fascinate me. Studying all the liberal sciences, the arts, the natural sciences . . . everything is just so fascinating to me, and I have this urge to know it all. Plus, in these colder months, I feel a little guilty being up in the library most of the time."

"Oh, I understand that last part. It is similar to the climate I am used to in New York, but definitely colder. Glad I have my warm coat and hat!" Jarek said with a smile. "So what is your favorite thing to read about or learn?"

"Well, for novels, I love a good suspenseful story, and for other topics, probably a three-way tie between studying animals, astronomy, and psychology."

"Well, that certainly is the full gambit of interests."

"Obviously, hence why I get consumed by books," Annie replied with a hint of playfulness.

Jarek wanted to ask her more about Martin, so he was debating in his mind if now was the right time. He knew that he needed to talk more with each person in an attempt to gain greater insight on all people involved. Perhaps, through talking, he could discover who the cards were referring to last night. He decided it was worth the risk of making Annie angry to help find the answers he needed.

"Annie, I know you likely are tired of people asking you questions right now, but would you be willing to talk for a bit about what happened here?"

"I wondered how long it would take for you to ask me questions," Annie responded in a cold manner, similar to that in which Rose always talked to him. She took a deep breath followed by a slightly audible sigh. "I guess you are here to help, and I should be willing to talk with you. It is appreciated, though I know I might not show it."

"I do understand that, Annie. Truly, I do. I have experienced great loss due to terrible circumstances."

"Well, perhaps we have more in common than I figured I would with a New York man."

"Perhaps, Annie," Jarek responded with a smile, grateful she seemed receptive to the conversation ahead.

"Well, before we talk, I should make sure our mess from breakfast is cleaned up, and we should go to a more comfortable room."

"Certainly, what room are you thinking? And I certainly can help clean this up."

"Let's meet in the parlor. The fireplace is usually already started by now in there." She paused and then slowly shifted her eyes to the kitchen door, then back at Jarek. "Ha, I won't be cleaning it myself, but I will make sure the staff gets it clean."

Annie responded with a tone that almost mocked Jarek for offering to help, because he should know better. They were a well-to-do family with hired help, after all.

"Oh," Jarek replied, caught off guard with her tone. "That sounds perfect. I will go to the parlor and wait for you."

"Perfect. I won't be long."

Annie stood up from her chair and walked to the kitchen. Jarek sat for a brief moment, got up, and moved from the dining room to the foyer. As soon as he entered the foyer, he swore he could faintly hear the piano in the parlor being played again. He walked slowly across the room to the archway of the parlor. As soon as his eyes peered into the room, the music seemed to stop, and there was no one to be seen. The hair on his arms and neck began to stand slightly. Jarek knew he was not totally alone in that room.

Another gust of wind could be heard outside, so Jarek moved to the large picture window facing out the front of the house. He began watching the wind blow the large snowflakes. He closed his eyes, still feeling his hairs stand on end from the energy in the room. The right side of his face got very cold.

The image of the Tarot spread from the prior night appeared in Jarek's mind. All six cards. He began to feel cold, damp, clammy breaths on his right cheek. He maintained focus on the visual of the cards, but then he began to hear the inhale and exhale of this sickly breath. Jarek took a shallow breath himself, unnerved from the sound and feeling on his ear. He opened his eyes slowly. There, reflected in the window, was a faint figure of young man with long hair tied back and a somewhat gruesome tone to his skin.

The young man seemed to be trying to say something directly into Jarek's ear, but his mouth was not opening. The sound coming from the young man grew louder in his ear. The image came in clearer the louder the sounds got. Jarek could then see why the young man could not talk—his mouth was sewn shut. Suddenly, like a bolt of lightning, he disappeared as quickly as he had come.

Jarek swallowed the saliva that had been pooling in his mouth from being too nervous and trying to tune into the entity.

"Is everything all right?" Annie asked as she walked into the parlor.

"Oh, yes, yes, of course. Just looking at the cold wind outside and glad I don't have to deal with that in New York City very often," Jarek lied.

Annie moved over to the small sofa and sat down. She patted the seat next to her. "Here, come sit down."

"Of course," Jarek responded as he briskly walked over to join her.

"Now, I will answer any of your questions that you may have—unless they get too painful, of course."

"Oh, yes, certainly," Jarek replied.

"But first, before I share about myself, Mr. Videni, I need to know who I am even talking to. What is your story, and why on earth is a man like you here, all the way from New York City?"

Jarek was nervous about this question. He remembered how Martin had responded when he realized that Jarek was not brought in to investigate Sarah's death by the local authority. Also, Rose had been unwelcoming since he arrived on their front step. He did not know how Annie would take the news of why he was here. He also did not want to disclose too much about himself either. There were too many unknowns in this case, and he knew something dark seemed to be listening every chance it got.

"Well, where would you like me to begin, Annie?"

"Anywhere you wish, but you know I am an inquisitive soul, so if too little is shared, I will likely have a follow-up question," Annie answered with a joking snarky tone.

"Very well." Jarek settled a bit more into the spot on the sofa. "I was born twenty-eight years ago in New York City. My mother had me and raised me for several years before she passed away." Jarek took a pause. He never liked to discuss his mother's passing. "After she was gone, my grandmother took me in."

"Was your father not around?" Annie asked.

"No. No, he left my mother after learning she was with child. They were never married, and once he found out that I was growing inside her, he just disappeared. The only thing I have of his is his surname. My mother thought it best to give me his last name."

"Do you know anything about him?"

"Not really. My mother did not really like to talk about him. My mother was an only child, and her parents were long gone. It was my father's mother that took me in and raised me. So I am fine with having his surname, because I associate it with my grandmother who raised me instead anyway."

"That was very nice of her."

"Yes, I am so thankful for her. She is the kindest person I have ever met. Genuine, kind-hearted, and someone who has suffered much in life but always seemed to find the good in every situation placed before her." Jarek clearly started to retreat into the fond memories he had of her.

"Is she . . . Is she passed on?"

"She is still with me. If I am being honest, I can't imagine life without her being a part of it. She was the one who shared with me about my father, though there was not much to tell. She enjoys telling the stories of her childhood and even her family's history before coming to America. So I lived with her and worked where I could over the years to help her pay to keep food on the table. I live near her place in New York. The only time I don't see her is when I am working a case, and when I went to France during the war of course."

"Does she know you are here in Saint Paul now?"

"Oh, yes, I always keep her abreast of my travels. In fact, it is from her I learned—" Jarek paused in order to not talk about his true reason for being involved with cases such as this. "I learned . . . Well, many of my skills I learned from her."

"Really?" Annie asked skeptically.

"Oh, yes, she is . . . um . . ." Jarek searched for words. "A very intuitive person. She has always been great at finding clues and helping people."

The truth is that Jarek learned everything he knew about being in tune with spirits and entities from the other side of the veil from her. However, he knew that Annie would likely not be comfortable talking about Sarah's passing if she thought he was a kook.

"She has many skills. She is able to read people's body language magnificently, and she knows how to tell if someone appears to be lying and things like that. I am very grateful for it. I would not be where I am or, in fact, be the man I am today if it weren't for her and her mentoring."

"That is very touching, Jarek, honestly. I am glad she was there for you. If she had not been, you would have been all alone after your mother's passing. Unless of course your father had returned."

"I doubt that very much. Even though he was the son of my grandmother, she never spoke highly of him. Also, since he abandoned me, I am not sure I would have wanted him to come back either."

"Oh, that is true, but you never know. Some people can change."

"Yes, that is very true. Perhaps one day, my path will cross with his, but right now, I don't plan to go out of my way to make sure that happens."

"Oh, I agree with that approach," Annie replied with a gentle smile. "What were their names?"

"Oh, my father's name is David, and my grandmother's is Leona . . . Leona Videni."

"I have always loved the name Leona. One of the temporary teachers at the schoolhouse was named Leona when I was younger."

There was a short pause. Jarek's expression clearly showed he missed home and his grandmother. He certainly could use her insight on this situation.

"Anyway, I finished school, worked some jobs in New York where I could. Then they sent me to France during the war. After I came back, I devoted all of my time to helping people that need it. Those who have lost loved ones or have been abandoned by loved ones . . ." Jarek trailed off and the room returned to silence.

Annie, trying to move on past the bit of gloom, broke the silence. "Well, thank you for sharing with me, Jarek. I do greatly appreciate it."

Annie stood up, moved over to the fireplace, and put a few more logs on to help rewarm the room again. "Much better," she said as the flame grew bigger. "It seems much colder today." Annie came back to the sofa and sat down, adjusting the cardigan she was wearing over her dress.

"Yes, I agree. It is much colder than I am used to," Jarek responded jokingly.

Both sat there for a moment in the quiet. It was that uncomfortable moment when the people in the room know that something awkward was about to be discussed, but no one wanted to be the first to talk.

"Well, I guess it's my turn for questions from you," Annie said, finally breaking the silence.

"Ahem," Jarek responded, clearing his throat. "I guess so."

"Ha, go ahead. Ask away. I have nearly a half hour before I meet some friends to go downtown to do some holiday shopping."

"OK, well, I guess I really just want to hear what you have to say about your mother's passing. Share with me your account and thoughts on the matter," Jarek stated matter-of-factly.

"I assume you know how that evening went. I am sure you read up on it prior to arriving and already talked to my father?"

"Well, yes, to an extent. I know the gist of it from talking with others. I try to do my research."

"OK, good, you didn't seem like a dewdropper type of man."

"Thank you. I do take pride in my work and never want to be lazy in my duties."

"A very admirable quality in a man."

"Thank you."

"You're welcome," Annie responded while flashing a small smile to Jarek. Transitioning the conversation back to the subject at hand, Annie continued, "If I am being honest, I am not even sure where to begin with everything."

"Just wherever you would like. You can share things you feel are important leading up to your mother's passing or that night or after the events of that evening."

"The evening when she died is one that I will never forget, but there is so much surrounding that night and leading up to it and after that convinced me the evening was preventable."

Jarek was surprised at what he just heard spoken from Annie's mouth. "Preventable?"

"Yes. I do not have proof, and I do not know the details, but I have witnessed too many oddities over this year. I know using the word *oddities* is facile and not very enlightening, but I will say something inside me tells me this wasn't all random acts."

"Maybe just start at the beginning of when you started to notices these . . . oddities."

Annie readjusted herself in how she was sitting on the sofa, taking a more comfortable position.

"All right. Well, this entire year seems to have been a giant mess of chaos. It seemed to start wonderfully. Father's business had just finished its busiest year ever. Mother had become so involved in the community, volunteering to help the poor, teaching piano, and becoming a prominent member of her spiritualism group. I finished my last few months at Central High School, hoping to go to college the following autumn. My parents would throw their social bashes for all their friends about once a month. I would get to spend a few hours dancing those nights and still be able to either hang out with my friends or go back upstairs to the library and read for the rest of the evening. It was the perfect year."

Annie brushed a tear that was beginning to form in the corner of her eye.

"I know. It is hard to think back on good times when dealing with troublesome times," Jarek stated empathetically.

"During early spring, around April, I believe, things started to change around here. My father began his sleepwalking habits fairly regularly, and he said he was beginning to have terrible dreams."

"Did he say what he dreamt about?" Jarek asked.

"He said it was about past events as a kid that scared him to death. He never went into great detail with me, but it was plain to see he was troubled. He said he needed to fix something. He needed to right a wrong. Well, anyway, my mother, of course, right away thought she knew the best way to help him. She would tell me that she wanted to be a medium for him to help make contact with the demons that haunted his past. So my father agreed, and they invited some of their closest friends over for a night of mediumship. They held it late at night. I was already in bed for the evening, so I do not know what all occurred or transpired. However, I do know that whatever had been trying to reach out from within him was completely awoken that night.

"Father seemed so different afterward. Sure, his sleepwalking became less frequent, but that was about all for improvement. He seemed to be gone from home much more, to get angry more easily, and mid-conversation he would go almost into a blank dream state, and he became very harsh . . ." Annie's voice drifted off. "He became so harsh toward my best friend—I do not know why. He was just a young man, and I know it is not conventional for a young man and woman to always be together if not courting, but there was no reason to be angry. Nothing romantic at all was occurring. Oh, how I hated the way he would talk to him or about him. Anytime Mother or I would attempt to explain to Father that the way Father spoke was unkind, he would get even madder.

"Then Samuel, my friend, um . . . Well, he decided to move on from here . . ." Annie trailed off for a moment. "Father mellowed some after that, but there was still so much anger. Now since mother's death, he seems to barely act like that, and he almost . . . Well, to be frank, he seems to barely show sorrow around me at all."

Jarek handed Annie a handkerchief to dab the tears streaming from her eyes.

"I'm sorry, I just miss Mother and Samuel so much, and I hate when my mind goes down this path of thinking that Father might have had something to do with it."

Annie placed her face in the handkerchief and began to cry heavier. Jarek's mind had many thoughts going through it about everything Annie had just disclosed to him. He wondered what happened the night when they tried to talk to spirits on the other side of the veil. He wondered what was happening to Martin and what caused his animosity to Annie's friend Samuel. Finally, Jarek's mind wondered if it was possible that the kind man who had shown him so much hospitality could be Sarah's true killer. These thoughts continued in his mind for a few moments before he realized Annie was still in tears.

"I am sorry for all this pain, Annie. Truly I am."

"Thank you, Jarek," Annie responded as she reached her hand out and placed it on top of the hand Jarek had resting on his knee. Looking directly into his eyes, her demeanor shifted slightly, and her eyes had the look of pure sadness and terror simultaneously. "I am so glad you are here. I hope you are able to help me."

"I will do my best, for you and for your family."

Annie sat straight up, adjusted her cardigan, and wiped her eyes dry.

"Thank you. Well, I should be heading downtown. I have lots to do today."

She stood up to leave the room, so Jarek stood up, too, as it was the courteous thing to do.

"Certainly. Enjoy your day, Miss Annie," Jarek said with a small smile.

Stopping at the archway, Annie turned back toward Jarek, looked at him, and tucked some loose strands of hair behind her ear.

"Thank you again. I am looking forward to having you here for the holiday."

"So am I," he responded.

She turned and left. He did genuinely mean that he was glad to be there for the holiday, but likely for a different reason than Annie seemed to think. He was excited to see all of them together and read the different dynamics between everyone in this house.

"Well, time to go find the good doctor," Jarek said quietly to himself. He ran upstairs quickly to gather his coat and hat so he could walk to Rice Park with some form of warmth wrapped around his body.

CHAPTER 6

THE DOCTOR

December 21, 1924, 11:25 a.m.

When arriving at Saint Paul Union Depot, Jarek recalled seeing signs outside pointing to Rice Park. He didn't want to ask Annie or Rose where Rice Park was, because he didn't want them to know he was going to try and find this Dr. Monroe. So, he was glad he had noticed the signs the evening prior. He bundled up in his coat and hat and ventured outside, where the wind had died down, thankfully, but the large snowflakes were still falling from the sky. Jarek figured the best route was to simply walk back toward Union Depot. As he walked down the front steps of the O'Connell home, his attention was drawn over to the large statue of Pan. The stray cat he saw when he first arrived sat at the base of the statue looking at him. The cat seemed to have an expression that questioned why Jarek was leaving the warmth of the home and venturing out into this cold air.

"Me, too, me, too," Jarek said quietly, talking to the cat, followed by a small chuckle. "But I got to do this, mac," he said aloud as he started his walk to the park.

The route seemed to be quicker during the daylight. Jarek soon came to the grounds of the Cathedral of Saint Paul. He noted the statue of the angel he had seen the entity peering from just the night prior. He could not see or hear anything out of the ordinary now, but he did have a sense of calmness and peace that was truly comforting to him after the pandemonium he had been experiencing since arriving in Saint Paul.

After passing the cathedral, Jarek turned and headed directly toward Saint Paul Union Depot. He realized how quiet it was while out walking as the snow fell to the ground. Even though snow already covered most of the city, and more was falling from the sky, the sounds from other people and automobiles were muffled and dampened. The sounds had nothing to echo off once absorbed by the snow, so it was so peaceful even though Jarek could see the busy, everyday lives of people in a growing city was still occurring.

As Jarek walked, he continued to admire the buildings and architecture intertwined with the natural landscapes, intermittent with areas where he could see the Mississippi River. It took him a bit to realize what people were doing sitting on stools on the ice that was covering the river. Jarek concluded they must be fishing through little holes cut in the surface.

Jarek could see Union Depot a tad further down the street from where he was walking. A sign for Rice Park caught his eye. It had an arrow pointing him north. When he turned, he could see the park only a few blocks farther, so he just kept trudging through the snow-dusted walkways.

The sign at the entrance of Rice Park was in full view. The quaintness of the park, which was more of a square than a park, gave

Jarek a smile. The city block was beautiful and well-laid-out. Immediately to his right was a beautiful library made of gray sandstone, and on the far side, he could see a beautiful Romanesque building made of pink granite and a red tiled roof. Jarek thought he could make out a sign from where he stood that this was the post office and courthouse. He continued walking directly into the park. It was fairly quiet, only a few people standing and sitting about chatting. Jarek exchanged a nod and greeting with a man who was walking through the park with a smaller dog. It was a breed that Jarek didn't recognize. Jarek brushed off some snow on a stone bench near a pine tree and sat down.

Sitting there, just observing his surroundings, Jarek began to let his thoughts drift about the O'Connell family. Each person he had the opportunity to talk with had been enlightening yet had brought more questions to his mind.

Rose clearly seemed to not be fond of Jarek, but he wondered if this was because she was tired of the invasion of their lives, or could it be that she didn't want him discovering anything connected to the case? He had difficulty reading her energy, which was unusual for him. However, he felt she truly did care about the family and was cold toward him because she was tired of them revisiting the painful memories. His ability to feel her energies was hard for him. His defenses went up fast with her because she came across so cold, yet on the inside, he felt she was a good person. She appeared as though she could be a friend if they'd met under other circumstances. Rose seemed to have cared deeply for Sarah, whose death had impacted her greatly. He could feel her grief and sadness at her core, but also there was something he was missing. Jarek knew that Rose was a key piece in the puzzle. He was just unsure of where she fit.

Jarek's mind moved to thoughts about Annie. Frankly, when he first met her, he felt she was rude, and clearly a very angry individual. However, he understood why. That rudeness and anger were likely fueled by her own way of mourning the loss of her mother. She clearly had animosity toward her father, and as she just disclosed earlier today, she believed that he could be involved with the tragedy. Jarek could not fathom how a child could think something like that about their own parent. Yet that belief had diminished the more Jarek thought about his own experiences in life and what he had seen. Annie appeared to have a good heart, loved to bring joy to others, and clearly seemed to fancy him, Jarek thought to himself. Maybe that was too presumptuous, yet she seemed to be a bit coquettish during their interactions today. He hadn't had much experience when it came to romantic feelings with another person in several years, so perhaps he was only imagining her actions in his head. He has always appreciated when people placed education in high regard, so he really liked to see her initiative and all of the encouragement for studies she received from her mother in the past, and Martin seemed to really like that characteristic of Annie's, too.

While thinking about Martin's encouragement of Annie, Jarek's mind moved on to Martin himself. He had been so welcoming to Jarek since their first meeting in the parlor. He was kind, seemed good-hearted and well-intentioned. He was athletic-looking, indicating he took care of himself to live a healthier life. Martin said he loved to ensure others were happy, and he seemed to want the best for his family. Rose seemed to maintain high regard for him, which was completely opposite of Annie's feelings. Martin was clearly struggling with something internally, and Jarek could tell that his mind was not in a good place. Jarek had seen cases in the same realm as what he witnessed with Martin last night. However, those cases were typically dealing with either an insane individual or an inhuman spirit that had infiltrated a human soul. Neither of which he initially felt was accurate in this situation.

Jarek knew there was darkness surrounding this case. He could feel the malevolence while in the house. The eyes watching him, the whispers in inaudible and inhuman sounds, and the shadows constantly whirling about when he turned corners in the house. It had not even been a full twenty-four hours, and he had already experienced so much. Yet Jarek was truly unsure of what he was experiencing. This force was either many spirits working in conjunction with one another, or it was truly a very strong force of darkness.

As Jarek sat on the stone bench, a shiver ran through his body. He looked up as he brought his mind back from his thoughts. He had been so deep in thought admiring the scenery while walking here and then thinking about the O'Connell family that he nearly forgot to really look using all his senses. He was so distracted by his own thoughts that he realized he was not alone on the bench. The energy emitting on the side of Jarek began to penetrate his body. He could see someone sitting there in his peripheral vision, a woman who was basically transparent. He assumed the woman was transparent due to having part of her in this world and part of her already on the other side of the veil. Jarek could tell she was a friendly being. She never once opened her mouth, but she began to communicate with him.

Many of the conversations Jarek had had with spirits was not a typical conversation. He had the ability to simply understand them, almost as if hearing their thoughts aloud. Sometimes he only heard them and felt a presence. Other times he could see some or all of them, and sometimes he had a full manifestation standing before him. As people walked through the park, to them it looked as though Jarek was simply sitting on the bench in silence. However, as he sat there, they had their own form of conversation. It was a peaceful, calm, and enlightening dialogue. He learned she was the same age as him, from Saint Paul, and was engaged to be married prior to her death. She was simply a woman who was a victim of tuberculosis and had passed a few months ago. She continued talking to Jarek for some time. She had a message she needed to give him so that he could then deliver to someone.

After a while, the energy began to fade away. Everything went silent for Jarek. He became in tune with the sounds of the city once again. The woman was gone—completely moved on to what awaited everyone beyond. He looked up and focused on the building on the other side of the street from the park. A sign hung above the door: DR. MONROE—PSYCHOLOGIST. Jarek stood up, smiling to himself as he walked across the park and street toward the doctor's office.

When Jarek arrived, he noticed BY APPOINTMENT ONLY painted on the door below the sign. Jarek figured he at least needed to see if he could make an appointment to meet with the doctor since he had walked all this way. He tried turning the knob on the door. The knob turned, but when he tried to open the door, it didn't budge. He knew instantly that the deadbolt was engaged. Likely meaning the doctor was not in. Jarek stood there for a moment contemplating what to do. He took a pad of paper and pencil from his coat pocket. He knelt down on one knee to write a note to leave for the office to give a telephone call for Jarek at the O'Connell home.

While he was kneeling down, something surprising caught his eye. Resting at the junction of the base of the building and the cobblestone walk, only about a foot away from him, he noticed a toad. It was just sitting there in the cold of winter.

"How strange . . ." Jarek whispered softly to himself as he was starting to reach down to touch it.

"May I help you sir?" said a voice coming from someone who had walked up to the side of Jarek as he was still kneeling.

Jarek looked up from the small critter to see an older gentleman standing there. A short man, completely gray head of hair, and bright green eyes behind wire rim glasses.

"Yes, eh, yes," Jarek responded, stumbling over his response. "I'm sorry, you just startled me . . . I was just going to leave a note for the office to reach me on the telephone when they reopened."

"Oh, quite all right. I didn't mean to make you jump," the man responded, moving in past Jarek. "And no need for a note . . . the doctor is in."

"Doctor? Dr. Monroe?" Jarek asked, feeling rejuvenated about his day.

"Yes, that would be me."

The doctor responded with a mix of sounding like he just wanted to get in his office to be out of the cold and also like he was a bit annoyed that someone was there unexpectedly with no appointment. Jarek could understand either reason for his tone.

"Well, don't just lollygag there. Come in out of the cold," Dr. Monroe said as he stood in the building holding the door for Jarek to enter.

As Jarek walked across the threshold, he glanced back down toward the toad. It was gone. In its place was a rock about the size of the toad, but it was definitely not a toad. Jarek shook his head in confusion and continued walking into the building.

Once inside the building, Jarek followed Dr. Monroe through the entryway and into the small sitting area. There was simply a coat rack, a few older-style chairs, and a small table with a few small medical booklets and newspapers lying on it. Only one small light hung from the ceiling, which added to the natural light coming in through the windows. However, it seemed as if no matter how sunny it was outside, this room was always dark and shadowy.

"I do have a patient coming in soon, but I would be happy to look at my scheduler to see when I can meet with you, Mister . . . ?"

"Videni. Jarek Videni," he replied quickly.

"Well, Mr. Videni, it will likely be after the holiday," Dr. Monroe stated as he retrieved a small book that had been sitting on a shelf next to the telephone that hung on the wall.

"Oh, no, I am not here to see you for a medical issue about myself," Jarek replied.

"Well, that injury on your wrist. You have been rubbing it since your arrival, and it seems to be saying otherwise," replied Dr. Monroe.

"Excuse me?" asked Jarek, confused.

"That injury there," he said, gesturing toward Jarek's wrist. "You've been holding it and rubbing it since I saw you. It looks to be irritated. But I am a psychologist, not a medical doctor."

Jarek looked down at his wrist confused. He hadn't realized he had been rubbing it. As he moved his hand away, he saw the irritation. At the direct center of the irritation were two small marks. Suddenly, the flash of the viper biting Jarek's arm in his dream from the night prior ran through his mind.

Jarek quickly pulled his coat sleeve down over his wrist.

"Oh, no—no, sir. I am not here for an appointment for myself," Jarek said.

"Well, sir, not to sound rude, but frankly, why are you here?"

"Yes, I am sorry to be an unexpected visitor. I didn't know I would be here today either when I first woke up," Jarek said, and he laughed a bit on the inside, because so many days he just had to see where the day took him. "I am just visiting the city, and something came up that I needed to ask you about."

"Well, it's a lovely city to spend the holiday."

"Actually, I am just here for the holiday, coincidentally. I am here to investigate the death of Sarah O'Connell."

The comment clearly caught Dr. Monroe's attention. He became stiff and totally silent. He continued looking down at the small appointment book without looking up.

"So, you are here to ask questions about Sarah?" Dr. Monroe asked in a rhetorical tone.

"Yes, sir. Well, sort of . . ." Jarek responded with some hesitation, trailing off.

"I am sure you have been given my statements on Sarah's medical history and her autopsy report?"

"Actually, I haven't. You see, Doctor, I am not your typical investigator. I am here to look at this case from, well, a . . . a different perspective."

Dr. Monroe gently closed his schedule book and looked up toward Jarek as he gave out a slight sigh. "So, you must be an acquaintance of her and her 'friends,' I assume," Dr. Monroe said skeptically.

"Excuse me? I am not sure what you mean, Doctor."

"Oh, I mean no offense. I have gotten to know the O'Connell household well over the years and hold them in very high regard. However, do I know that Mrs. O'Connell was involved with the spiritualist group here in the city."

"You don't think there is any validity to her beliefs? Or the beliefs held and experiences had by many people?" Jarek asked, trying to maintain a calm tone. Though he was somewhat annoyed that Dr. Monroe immediately began to jab at spiritualism.

"Please, don't take me wrong. I respect when people are religious and believe in God myself. I was raised Catholic as a boy after all. But . . . but I just don't agree with people being all consumed in this fad of spiritualism."

Dr. Monroe made a slight huff and shook his head a bit before continuing to share his opinion as Jarek stood there in silence, simply listening.

"I just think it isn't right to mislead people. All this silliness of people holding séances and talking to the dead. It makes a bunch of well-respected individuals end up looking like a bunch of Dumb Doras."

Dr. Monroe took a pause. He looked up at Jarek, whose face showed mild anger.

"Oh, I am sorry. Don't listen to this old fool. I spout off too much without thinking."

Jarek took a breath to cool down from the heat of anger bubbling inside him.

"Are you so close-minded, or rather so arrogant, that you believe the only reality is what you can see with your own eyes and is directly in front of you?" Jarek asked him with a hint of defensiveness in his voice.

"We have so much in the scientific world that is being discovered that when spiritualists get involved, it muddies the water and just confuses people. I believe it hinders the advancement of science. Look, Jarek, there is so much yet that mankind has yet to discover in the physical world, and so many questions yet to be answered. I am simply a man trying to find the answers to the unknown and the misunderstood."

"I understand your logic, Doctor. So, for the purpose of this meeting, I will keep my views on spiritualism to myself," Jarek said while looking directly at Dr. Monroe. "Oh, and don't worry . . . I won't try to convert you," he continued while giving a smirk, in hopes of lightening the mood in the room between the two men.

Dr. Monroe gave a slight chuckle back, understanding that Jarek was trying to disarm the slight hostility that was brewing between their differences of opinion.

"All right, Mr. Videni, what is it about the family that you wish to discuss?"

"Well, I was informed on the circumstances of Sarah's death. The gruesomeness of it. The fact that her heart had been removed. So, unless there is anything else about Sarah you would like to share, I actually have questions that pertain to Martin."

"Yes, Sarah's death was definitely more violent than any death I have ever seen."

"Seen?" Jarek asked.

"Yes. You see, the coroner here is a good friend of mine. He sometimes asks me to assist him when it is a more violent crime. He likes to have someone to lean on and help him mentally if the victim died from violent means. The autopsy was fairly difficult for me. Usually, I am able to disassociate with the individuals when my friend asks me to conduct an autopsy with him. However, Sarah's death was just too much. It took me many days after examining her body for me to get the gruesomeness of it out of my mind."

"Was there anything beyond the heart missing, Doctor?"

"There were three key things about her body that stood out. First, her throat had been cut—one clean swipe of a blade. Second, her heart was cut completely out. It was done with fairly good precision, too. Lastly, her eyes were wide open. They had a strange look of pain, sorrow, and horror all combined into one expression."

Dr. Monroe took a pause in order to maintain his composure.

"It is quite all right, Doctor. Take all the time you need."

"No, I am fine. It is just the look in her eyes that I will never forget. I keep hoping I'll never witness it again for as long as I walk this Earth."

"Many on this Earth have never seen something as horrific as you have witnessed. Sadly, many others have, or they have seen much worse. This world can be a cruel and dark place, but we must hold on to the light. Keep our hope alive in all that is good. That light can always chase away the darkness; we just have to let it and sometimes help it along."

"I suppose you're right, young man. It can just be very difficult when life keeps hitting you with a club multiple times in a year . . ." Dr. Monroe trailed off, becoming even more solemn.

"That is very true. I like to believe the trials we go through in life are intended to make us stronger. But I know that sometimes life is just cruel, and we must just continue on our path. Use our experiences from life as tools to overcome any future obstacles that may fall in that path."

Dr. Monroe wiped away a tear rolling down his cheek.

"OK, Mr. Videni, enough of this sadness. What other questions do you have for me today?" he asked.

"Well, I know that Martin is one of your patients. However, I am curious, if I may ask you—well, ask you if there is anything of concern you'd like to share or discuss?"

"Oh, no need to be coy with me. You are wondering if I would share my thoughts on Martin's—well, um, oddities?"

"Well, yes," Jarek responded, relieved that Dr. Monroe was a frank man. "I witnessed him acting very peculiar last night. He had been acting very warmly and welcoming since I had first arrived. Then suddenly, he seemed off and retired to his room for the evening. Then later on, I awoke to find he had sleepwalked to my room, and when I tried to awaken him, he became angry. Then—this was the strangest part—he said, "My name isn't Martin; my name is Peter." It just really startled me because he seemed wide awake when he said it."

"Normally, I wouldn't share very much information on a patient that I am still treating. However, I do believe that you need to hear my thoughts."

"It really would be most appreciated, Doctor."

"I can actually start at the beginning. I first began to treat Martin as a boy. He was thirteen years old the first time I saw him. He had just been in a horrific accident at the timber factory in a small town just east of here on the Saint Croix River. I don't remember all the details, but I do remember that his father let him work there during the summer in lieu of working at his print factory. Martin and his friend Peter worked directly in the river, helping maneuver the timber out of the water onto the shore. Something happened where Martin had fallen, and he got caught in the undercurrent. His friend Peter jumped in and rescued him, but then he in turn was swept away and never found. I happened to be visiting a friend in the area and was nearby when the workers pulled Martin to the shore. He was yelling for help. He has been my patient ever since."

"Very sad, but an interesting way to meet a lifelong patient," Jarek interjected.

"Yes. Well, ever since this incident he began to exhibit strange behaviors. His parents became increasingly concerned over the years. Then, after he married Sarah, she began to have the same concerns.

He would have strange shifts in temper. Sometimes these transitions would occur as quickly as snapping a finger. Other times, it seemed he would fade in and out of almost being another individual entirely."

"What did you think might be causing this in him?"

"His parents and Sarah all asked me, at different times, if I thought of the possibility that it was something caused by the Devil. Throughout history, it seems that blaming the Devil is the only option for something that can't be explained. However, as we have gained more knowledge in science and medicine, we have learned so much that can provide an explanation."

"What do you mean, Doctor?"

"Well, for instance, when I started working with Martin, I began to conduct much research on similar cases of people. People who seemed to have personality changes or act as if they are suddenly a different person, or they become very angry and aggressive for no reason. The more I met with Martin, the more he seemed to be so similar to the people having this illness I had read about. The theory among professionals is people who exhibit behaviors like this to have a diagnosable syndrome. They call it 'double consciousness.'"

Jarek had a look of confusion on his face.

"Think of it as two different personalities, distinct from one another, living within one person. Hence why many religious people automatically believe a person to be possessed by the Devil . . ." Dr. Monroe trailed off a bit because he realized his last statement might have come across as condescending to Jarek. "Oh, I am sorry. I just get frustrated when people have so little belief in the science of the world," he continued.

"No need to apologize. I, too, understand the feeling of many people questioning my work and research," Jarek replied with a smirk.

"That is a fair response," Dr. Monroe said with a small chuckle.

"So, Doctor, if they believe this to be a mental disorder, where does it come from? Is it treatable?"

"Well, some believe that these people are simply born with a predisposition to having double consciousness. Others believe that a life-changing traumatic event can cause it, because the mind creates a new personality to help handle and cope with the situation. I personally believe it is the latter. Now, as far as treating it, there was a French neurologist years ago, Dr. Jean-Martin Charcot, who believed in using hypnosis to treat his patients suffering from this issue. I have had my doubts on this, but hypnosis has been proven many times to help a person's troubled mind. I decided to try treating Martin with hypnosis."

"Did you see any progress?" Jarek asked.

"Well, I believe so. It seemed he was having fewer incidents of mood swings, or his mind turning to believe he was actually his boyhood friend Peter. I have treated him only a few times since April. I guess his family has gotten very busy over the summer and autumn. However, I fear that Sarah's passing and the gruesomeness of it might have returned him to an even worse state of mind than he had been previously."

"I can concur with him exhibiting those behaviors. Just last night in fact."

Dr. Monroe stood there with his hand on his chin, nodding gently out of concern for Martin.

"Nevertheless, I am new in the house and am not sure what all has occurred since Sarah's death. Annie seems to hide away in the library, Ms. Smith is consumed at ensuring the house is ran appropriately, and then besides last night, Martin seems like such an energetic man and full of life. With that said, I do know that Annie has concerns about her father. However, she seems to partake in the same belief system as Sarah had and questions if it's the Devil."

"Yes, I do believe she has gotten somewhat involved with the spiritualist community here. Also, I don't believe that they shared with Annie my diagnosis and treatment of Martin. So naturally, I would assume that with her shared beliefs of her family and companions, Annie would automatically believe that Martin's behaviors could be caused by something . . . something from the other side. I'm not surprised she could link that to Sarah's unfortunate end either."

"But you don't believe he could have turned violent toward Sarah?" Jarek asked him bluntly.

"I don't believe he would. For you see, in all of the research that has been done on individuals around the world who are treated for double consciousness, they are no more violent than any other common person.

"Even renowned phycologist Dr. Morton Prince up in Boston has studied individuals with similar diagnoses and has concluded that it is a medical condition. He fully supports the theory that double consciousness does not change someone's behavior to be inherently violent. Though we have yet to discover a cure, it can be treated, as I said earlier. Frankly, it could be more common than we think, because these people are no different than you or I. They just have a mind that handles significant events different than we do. It is neither their choice nor desire to cope with events in such a way; it is simply the way it is."

Jarek stood there with more questions, knowing that there was the possibility of Martin either being at the core of the tragedy or simply being a man in need of help as a victim himself. Though Jarek thought perhaps it was both of these options.

"Please, young man, do not think differently of Mr. O'Connell knowing this information."

"No, sir, I have no intention of thinking of him in a negative manner over something like this. I myself have plenty of things going on in my head that I know others would judge me harshly for. The last thing I want to do is judge someone for simply . . . Well, simply being different," Jarek responded with a sympathetic tone.

"Thank you. I appreciate that as a medical professional and as a human," said Dr. Monroe.

There was a moment of silence and then a tap on the door. The door began to open slowly, and a young woman came in.

"Ah, Ms. Walsh! Right on time," said Dr. Monroe.

"I'm sorry, Doctor, am I intruding?" the woman asked in a gentle and kind voice.

"No, no. This young man was just on his way out. If you'd like, you can go straight into the office, and I will be there in a moment," Dr. Monroe said while gesturing to the half-open door just beyond the lobby.

"Thank you," she replied as she walked past the gentlemen. They both gave her a nod, signaling a silent good day to her.

As soon as she was past them and in the office, Jarek knew it was time to be on his way.

"I cannot thank you enough, Doctor. I appreciate your time and for discussing this matter."

"It was my pleasure, Jarek. I enjoyed meeting you, and I do hope you are able to help the family and bring them peace. They are such a good family, and no one deserves to go through something like they have."

Jarek looked down and nodded in concurrence with the significance of the tragedy. He slowly looked up at Dr. Monroe to say farewell.

"Before I go, Doctor, I do have something I need to share with you."

Dr. Monroe responded with a look of befuddlement.

"Now, I know you said you're not a religious or spiritual man, and you probably would question much of what I believe. But, I must tell you something."

Jarek took a pause before continuing.

"Elizabeth misses you very much. She does not want you to continue to blame yourself for not being able to help her. It was a sickness beyond healing. The tuberculosis was just too much, and the collapsed lung therapy just didn't work. She appreciated you as a father and never would have traded you for anything in the world. She asks you to give her mother a hug for her. Also, tell Marcus that though they did not get the chance to wed and build a life together, she wishes him the best in life, and she knows that one day he will become almost as good of a father as the one she had. Elizabeth says it is OK to continue to grieve, but it is also time to start the healing process for yourselves."

Dr. Monroe stood there in awe of what Jarek just said. After what felt like several minutes, he finally was able to muster up a few words. "How . . . how do you know all that?" He asked Jarek, clearly shaken.

"Well, Doctor, there is so much yet that mankind has yet to discover in the spiritual world and so many questions yet to be answered. I guess we are simply both men trying to find the answers to the unknown and misunderstood."

"Thank you, Jarek. Truly, thank you. You be sure to look after that bite on your wrist."

Jarek nodded his head toward the doctor, who stood there with a tear rolling down his cheek. Jarek turned and walked out to venture back toward the home that he hoped held the answers to the unknown awaiting him.

CHAPTER 7

THE BOOK

December 21, 1924, 4:36 p.m.

The temperature seemed to be a tad warmer on Jarek's face as he journeyed along the walk back toward the O'Connell residence. It was not nearly as warm as the winter air he was used to in New York, but it was the warmest it has felt on his cheeks since arriving in Saint Paul. He was nearing the walk-up to the house when he felt an internal nudge to take a pause where he stood. Jarek looked up the drive toward the home, once again admiring the beauty of it. The elegance and grandeur of the estate. The trees, the rooftop, and the statue of Pan dusted with snow was truly a remarkable sight. It was clear to Jarek why Martin took such pride in his home.

Jarek was unaware of how much time had passed. It could have been minutes, or it could have been nearly an hour. His mind was so deep in thought. Jarek was contemplating everything he had heard and observed since arriving. As he stood there, his eyes began to refocus on the present and were once again looking at the home. • Jarek sensed something watching him. It was similar to the feeling he had in the foyer of the home. He began to scan the grounds with his eyes. The feeling was projecting directly from the home. Jarek was about to take a step up the walk when his eyes were drawn to the windows of the library. As he gazed up at the second story windows, he could see the drapes unnaturally slightly pulled to the side. The energy exuded from whatever entity was watching Jarek from behind those windows. It was attempting to make a full apparition but seemed to be struggling to concentrate its maximum energy.

"Excuse me, sir?"

The quiet, timid male's voice broke Jarek's concentration on the window. He turned to where the voice had been coming from.

"Yes, may I help you?" Jarek asked as his mind began to refocus on the person standing in front of him only to find a familiar face. "Well, hello!" Jarek said as he gave a small smile to the young man he remembered from the Saint Paul Union Depot.

"Hello, J. V.," replied the young man. "I'm sorry, sir, but you only signed the note at the train depot with initials."

"Ah, yes, that's right. Please, call me Jarek."

"Jarek. Well, it is a pleasure to formally meet you. I realize that last time, when I made small talk with you, you were . . . well, you were preoccupied with . . . something."

"Yes, I was a bit *preoccupied*. Sorry about that."

"Oh, please don't apologize. Because of you, they were able to help lay a man's body to rest. You don't have to explain yourself to me, and you certainly have no need to apologize to me or anyone for what you . . . what you are able to do."

"Thank you . . . ?" Jarek drew out the inflection to indicate the young man never formally introduced himself.

"Hamish. My name is Hamish. Sorry about that."

"And you, Hamish, have no need to apologize either," Jarek replied with a smile to help put the young man's apparent nervousness at bay.

"Thank you, Jarek."

As they stood there on the walk, the stray cat walking around near the front steps of the O'Connell home caught Jarek's eye. Then his eyes shifted quickly back toward the window of the library, then back toward Hamish.

"So, Hamish, not to sound too forward, but what can I do for you? I know that you running into me here is no coincidence."

"You really can read minds," Hamish responded sarcastically.

"Oh, no, some days I wish I could read minds. Then other days I am very glad I don't have that ability."

"No, no. I suppose that would be quite loud and a bit invasive of people's personal lives."

"Quite true, Hamish. Believe me, my life is loud enough, and I see enough already. I don't need mind reading to be added on top of that."

Hamish gave a small chuckle, still clearly nervous to be talking to Jarek. "So, on that subject, may I ask you, how you did know that poor man's body was hidden out of sight?"

"I don't know if you are ready to hear all that, Hamish. However, let me just say that I have . . . well, I have certain abilities and gifts. I try my hardest to use these gifts to help those that need it. It can be as simple as passing along a message to a loved one, or it can be like my current challenge facing me. Hopefully, helping this family solve the mystery that haunts them," Jarek said in a figurative and literal manner.

"I am certain they are very appreciative of your assistance during this time."

"Thank you. I just truly hope I can help them." Jarek's thoughts drifted off for a moment as he looked back at the O'Connell home. "Now, Hamish, you are here for a reason. I know it wasn't just to ask about the gentleman at the train depot. That much is clear. What can I do for you?" Jarek asked as he began to try and determine what piece Hamish was in this puzzle.

"To be blunt, I may be somewhat . . . involved," Hamish replied skittishly.

"Excuse me?" Jarek responded, confused.

"Well, you see . . . May we sit down here?" Hamish asked while gesturing to some of the large rocks right off the walkway.

"Of course," Jarek responded.

Both of the men brushed some snow off the rocks and then proceeded to sit down facing the street, backs toward the O'Connell home.

"I should rephrase myself. I am not involved with the death of Mrs. O'Connell by any means. However, I do have a slight relationship with the family. I have been in the home once. This past June. I was there when Miss O'Connell, Annie, asked me to join her for . . . well, for a séance. She wanted to talk to someone that we both had known. He died in the house only a month prior to then."

Hamish grew very quiet as a tear began to roll down his cheek.

"What happened that night, Hamish? The night you visited Annie," Jarek asked sternly.

"Well, it was late at night. Annie had asked me to meet her at the back door of the home at midnight. When I got there, she was waiting outside. I could tell she was even more anxious than I was. She was already in her nightgown, hair hanging down and brushed for the night. I assume she had pretended to get ready for bed as to not give her parents an inkling of anything from her normal routine.

"I remember, as soon as she saw me, she came right over and said, 'It's about time.' Even though I don't recall being late. Anyway, she told me I had to be absolutely quiet and follow her. We went into the home, through the kitchen, then the ballroom, out to the stairs in the foyer. We went upstairs to the second floor, and right as we were about to walk down the hallway, I remember she grabbed my hand

and rushed us into the room on the left. She said it was because she could see her father walking down the hallway."

Jarek was visualizing the home while Hamish shared the story with him, knowing instantly that they must have gone into the guest room where he had been staying. His mind continued to almost go in a trance while Hamish was speaking. The energy was drawing him into the past to see what happened.

"Once we were in the bedroom, I asked Annie where we were going. She responded that we needed to get to the library without being seen. She walked past the bed over to the corner of the room. She pushed slightly on the wall, and a small door opened, revealing a passageway to another room. She grabbed my hand, and we moved through the passageway to a dead end. Annie pushed on the wall there, opening another door that led directly into the library. The room was dark except for several candles that were lit throughout the room. She moved quickly across the room to nearly where the windows are," Hamish explained as he turned slightly, gesturing toward the library windows on the second story.

Jarek turned, looking up at the windows. He saw the entity there in its full form now watching them talk outside. It was the spirit of the young man from earlier. Mouth sewn shut, looking ghastly and scared. Behind the figure lurked a very dark presence. Jarek could not make it out, but the energy resonating from it made him nauseated inside.

"I could see that Annie had already drawn something on the floor. A symbol of some sort."

"What symbol?" Jarek asked.

"I . . . I don't remember."

"Please try," Jarek said as he placed his hand on Hamish's shoulder.

"I honestly don't remember. I just recollect it was like nothing I had ever seen. A strange circle, with some designs within. Annie sat in the center of it and told me to sit right outside of it. I held her hands as she began to close her eyes and mumble something to herself. I . . . I don't know how to explain what happened next."

"Just try, Hamish. Trust me, it takes an awful lot to shock me."

"All right. Well, as Annie kept mumbling, the candles she had lit in the library began to flicker violently until most of them went out. I remember the air in the room became heavy, musty, and then began to outright stink. Then . . . I don't know how else to say it, but suddenly behind Annie, I swear . . . I swear I saw Samuel, our friend. He looked very scared. It looked as if he were about to say something, then I heard a very loud noise . . . then poof."

"Poof?" asked Jarek.

"We blacked out for several minutes. When I came to, I found Annie on the floor just awaking as well. The room was silent and felt like it had returned to normal. I asked her what happened. I'll never forget what she said: 'What needed to be done, is done.' She had a cold, dark look in her eyes. Then suddenly, she looked right at me and smiled. Then Annie said I had better be going. She led me out the door, down the hall, and out the front door. She simply told me to have a good night and then shut the door to the house."

"That's all she said? Nothing about what you had seen?"

"Well, I don't know if Annie saw Samuel or not. I think that whatever happened scared her too much. She probably never wants to talk about it again. I believe she did see him, but this is her way of dealing with it. I don't . . . Does that make any sense?"

"Yes, everyone has their own ways of dealing with intense or traumatic situations."

"Well, I better be going. It's nearly time for me to get to the train depot to help with the dinner patrons."

"Thank you, Hamish, for sharing this all with me. It means a lot that you trust me with this information."

"Well, I knew I could trust you Jarek, and I knew that you would be understanding. I just wanted you to know that . . . that something in that house isn't right. And I believe that, somehow, what I saw that night is connected to the death of Mrs. O'Connell. Well, thanks again," Hamish said as he stood up and began to walk back from the direction he had come.

While standing up, Jarek shouted back, "Thanks again! If you happen to remember that symbol or anything else, please let me know!"

"I will," Hamish responded while looking back at Jarek with a smile and hand wave.

Jarek turned back toward the house. He looked once more up at the library window and saw the figures still standing there. Then, whatever darkness lurked behind the young man suddenly engulfed him, and they both vanished. Jarek ran up the front walk and rushed through the front doors.

"Excuse you, Mr. Videni. We just had these floors cleaned," said Rose as she stood in the foyer, clearly annoyed at his carelessness for tracking snow and mud in.

"Oh, gosh, Ms. Smith. I am so sorry. That was very senseless of me."

"It certainly was," Rose replied as she turned and walked toward the kitchen. "I will send someone out to clean that up."

"Excuse me, Ms. Smith," Jarek said to get her attention.

"Yes, Mr. Videni?"

"Where is Miss Annie?"

"I'm sorry, she is out for the remainder of the day. Along with Mr. O'Connell. She is still out shopping, and Martin is at the print factory. They should be back before dinner though."

"Thank you . . . Ms. Smith." Jarek responded, with a tone of confusion to his voice.

"Of course. Go ahead and retire to the library, Mr. Videni. We will wait for Mr. O'Connell to come home before we eat, so dinner will not be for several hours. You should go rest or read," Rose said before turning and continuing on to the kitchen.

After hearing what young Hamish had to say, Jarek was sure that he would find Annie, Martin, or Rose up in the library at this very moment. He was certain one of them must have some part in this, but he did not know what it could be. However, now that neither Annie nor Martin was not in the house, and Rose was downstairs, Jarek felt as if he were as far along in this investigation as when he first crossed the threshold the day prior.

Standing there in the foyer, Jarek decided to take Rose's advice and venture upstairs to the library. He did want to have some time in there himself to seek out any clues that might be beneficial in any way. He meandered up the stairs and down the hall when he remembered what Hamish had told him. He stopped and went into his room to find the hidden door that joined his room to the library.

While he opened the door to his room, he began to visualize Annie and Hamish the night they tried to contact their friend Samuel. He walked across his room to the far corner. Jarek looked at the elaborate woodwork that covered the walls, but he couldn't see the outline of an apparent passageway. He began to push slightly on the area of wall that Hamish said Annie opened that night. Then Jarek pushed on a corner trim piece that had an unusual seam. It released a latch, and sure enough, it opened like a door to reveal a small passageway through the wall. It was short, maybe five feet at the most, Jarek estimated. When he got to the other end, he could see the handle that likely opened that door. He slowly turned it and it opened, too. He walked through the opening into the library. The room was gloomy, as most of the draperies were drawn. Small beams of light came into the room from the small openings in the center of each window where the drapes met.

Jarek began to wander around the room to see if he could find anything unusual or out of place. At first glance, nothing looked or felt unusual to him. He moved over to the windows that faced the front of the home. There was a small sitting area with two chairs, a side table, and a lamp.

Jarek looked down at the floor where Hamish said Annie had drawn the symbol. However, there was a large Persian carpet laying there. He knelt down and began to roll back the carpet to see if it was covering the symbol Annie had allegedly scribed on the floor.

To his dismay, the floor appeared blank. Knowing what Annie drew on the floor in her attempt at contacting their friend could help answer many questions. Jarek stood up and began to try and feel the energy of the room. Whatever apparition and entity that stared out at Jarek and Hamish from this room earlier seemed to have gone.

The library seemed to have a comforting feeling to it now. Jarek understood why both Sarah and Annie seemed to find their solace in here. He glanced over to the stairs where Sarah had come to her tragic death. It still felt as if hardly anything had been revealed to him yet in solving this case. A wave of hopelessness and disappointment rolled over Jarek.

Suddenly, a small glow began to form at the base of the staircase. A small flicker of light moving ever so slightly. It began to grow into an orb about the same size that appeared during dinner the night prior. Jarek began to think he knew who this orb was by focusing his mind and energy toward it as it grew.

"Sarah, I need your help. I can't do this without you. I need your help in order to help you," Jarek said while concentrating all his energy on the orb.

There didn't seem to be a response from it. *Perhaps it isn't Sarah*, Jarek thought to himself.

"Please, I need you to assist me in this investigation," Jarek pled while talking aloud to the entity hovering near the stairs.

Jarek stood there, breathing shallow. He wanted to be patient but was getting anxious to find the answers he desperately needed. The orb began to back away from Jarek. At first, he thought it must be fading away, unable or unwilling to muster enough energy to maintain contact with him. Then Jarek realized it was beginning to actually move up the staircase to the loft in the library. He knew he must follow it up there.

Jarek slowly moved up the staircase toward the loft. The orb was gently floating, so he did not want to appear to rush it as he followed close in step. As Jarek breached the top of the stairs, he saw a lovely loft designed to be a study area. Two comfy-looking chairs, a small desk, and several side tables stacked with books and notepads. The loft extended halfway around the room to the left, allowing access to the two-story bookcases in the room.

As soon as Jarek reached the top of the stairs and stood in the loft, the orb suddenly seemed to dissipate and fade away.

Standing there in the loft, Jarek knew something of importance must be there. He simply needed to uncover it. He wished the entity that showed him the loft was still there to help guide him. Jarek began to look around the space, seeing what books were stacked and perusing the notes lying about the space. He observed many religious texts and many books in other languages, so he wasn't positive on their subject matter. Jarek grabbed a book that seemed to be centered on the desk as if recently read. He began to flip through the pages and realized it was in Greek. However, after a few moments, he began to see symbols on the pages. He quickly realized he was skimming through one of the texts of Solomon. The Hebrew king that claimed to have learned the many mysteries of the supernatural. Jarek's most educated guess, by studying the words he understood and recognizing the symbols, was that it was a copy of *The Lesser Keys of Solomon*. It appeared that Mrs. O'Connell studied not only being a spiritualist but also the history of angels and demons.

Jarek himself has studied this very topic in order to gain a better understanding of the world surrounding him. He found that by studying more, he was better able to understand the many entities that he had encountered or could encounter.

Jarek continued to flip through the pages in the book when he noticed that one page was dog-eared. It was the section titled

"Shemhamhorash." He had read this section before. It covered the information on the various demons and their seals that King Solomon claims to have conjured, learned from, and controlled. It was a fascinating read. One could learn about the many entities that plague and wreak havoc in the world and the other side of the veil. This knowledge made it easier for someone to know what dark forces they were dealing with, and once they know which entity it was, it was easier to rid them from this world. However, Jarek learned years ago that some people use this knowledge in a twisted manner. They try to use these entities for their benefit. But they do not realize that all deals with these beings come at a price. Jarek just needed to determine if Sarah had been learning this information for knowledge expansion, or was it to bargain and make a deal?

Jarek perused more pages in the book, looking at the various seals of each high-profile demon. He began to study their seals. Suddenly, it occurred to him that one of these seals could be the symbol that young Hamish had partially remembered seeing the night he and Annie tried contacting their friend.

Jarek decided to refamiliarize himself with the various symbols, so he proceeded to move to one of the chairs and sat down. As he paged through the book, it became clear to him that this book was fairly old and had been paged through many times before. The binding was worn, and the pages turned brown from both the touch of human fingers and time itself.

Some time had passed when Jarek realized it was dark outside. He closed the book and rested it on his lap. He tilted his head on the top of the wingback chair. His eyes grew heavy, so he closed them for a brief moment. Jarek's mind began to wander and process all the conversations he had had so far, going deeper and deeper into an almost dreamlike trance while feeling everything surrounding him. The up and down of his chest slowed to a shallow pace as his body began to drift into sleep.

"How could you two do something like this?" asked a woman in a sharp manner.

Jarek's eyes opened wide as his quickly stood up startled. He moved to the edge of the railing near the staircase and looked down upon the library. There in the middle of the room stood Sarah. Next to her stood another person whose back was facing toward Jarek. Jarek's eyes were focused narrowly on the people standing there. The surroundings of the library began to fill with a dark misty haze. A thick black fog was filling the entire space during this heated discussion that Jarek was somehow witnessing.

"We had to. There was no other option!" the second person shouted.

Jarek did not recognize the voice. It seemed muffled and distorted. Jarek's eyes kept seeming to fade away and forced him to refocus. It was different than a typical dreamlike state. He realized he was in more of a memory instead of a dream. Someone or something was showing him an event of the past.

The voice Jarek was not familiar with continued.

"We had to try. He needed to come back to us. He needed to know that we loved him and that he was one of us."

"He was one of us. He is beyond this world now. Anything that is here now is not truly him. You bound his spirit to this house; he is stuck between the here and the beyond," Sarah said.

"Yes, but at least he is with us."

"You foolish child. That is not what is best. His loss was a tragedy, but he must be allowed to move on. Whatever dark craft you used, it not only bound his spirit to the house, but he was truly brought back by something darker and more sinister than you can ever imagine. How could you be so foolish?"

"I'm not foolish! I know more of what I am doing than you realize. This is for the best, for all of us."

"How could you know what is best for all of us? I thought I knew you both, but clearly you have gone astray on your own. I pray you see the light, but I am not sure I can help you until you are ready to undo what has been done."

"Oh, there is nothing to undo. There is only more to be done. You'll see, Sarah. You'll see," replied the person before they dashed out of the library, leaving Sarah standing there. She was clearly trying to hold back from crying.

"Oh, Samuel, I am so sorry. Sincerely sorry. I will do everything within my power to help you. If you can hear me, know that I love you. I am here for you, and I promise I will help you pass back over to the next life."

Jarek began to move his way slowly down the staircase to get closer to Sarah. As he reached the bottom of the stairs, Sarah looked directly toward him.

Jarek froze.

Can she see me? Is that even possible? Jarek wondered to himself.

"Samuel, I can feel you here. Please let me know it's you."

Suddenly, Jarek felt something pass through him. His entire body felt like needles pricking him over every inch of his body. The energy that passed through him began to fully take shape. As it became more visible, it revealed a young man. A young man with shoulder-length hair and a thin build. The young man seemed familiar to Jarek.

"Samuel, please, I need to know you're here," said Sarah.

It dawned on Jarek that she couldn't see the boy the same way that he could. She could likely feel his energy but not see it. Then it hit Jarek—the young man . . . Jarek had seen him before. This was the same person that revealed himself to Jarek in the parlor. However, the boy didn't appear as gruesome, and his mouth was not sewn shut. There must have been some event that led to this boy's spirit changing from what Jarek was seeing now and what Jarek's eyes witnessed in the parlor.

"Mrs. O'Connell," the young man tried to vocalize, but it was barely audible.

It was hard to hear even for Jarek, who could see the spirit's mouth move.

"Mrs. O'Connell!" The spirit said louder, but with no luck of Sarah hearing him.

Sarah wiped away a few tears. As a medium, she could sense the spirit of the young man but couldn't see him, which caused her much frustration, Jarek assumed. She turned as if to leave the library.

"Mrs. O'Connell!" the young man exclaimed. The sheer energy of the spirit trying to make contact created a shockwave through the room, causing Sarah to enclose her arms around her stomach as a natural reaction.

A lamp on the side table fell off, and several books fell from the bookcases.

"Samuel! Oh, Samuel!" Sarah responded. "I knew it was you," she said, as the young man had gained enough energy to finally reveal himself to Sarah.

"Mrs. O'Connell, I need your help."

"Samuel, what have you done?" Sarah said with so much sadness in her voice. "Why did you do it?"

"I didn't think I had any other option. I wasn't right in the head, Mrs. O'Connell. I would never be normal and be able to fit into your world."

"Why would you say that, Samuel? We have been here for you through it all. We loved you no matter what."

"I know that now. I just didn't realize it at the time. It is too late for me, I can't come back. I moved on once . . . I let myself move on, no matter how painful it was for those around me."

The spirit took a pause. Jarek shifted his eyes between the young man and Sarah.

"But, Mrs. O'Connell . . . they brought . . . they brought me back. It was against my will, and I can't figure out how to leave."

This was the first time that Jarek witnessed a spirit showing physical emotion. The boy was indeed crying. Tears rolled down the cheeks of the spirit with a crystal-like shine.

"I know, Samuel. I am going to help you move on from this place. You no longer belong here. Your time on this Earth has passed." Sarah paused to brush more tears away from her own face. "Oh, my boy, you must be so scared, so confused. I believe . . ."

Sarah continued to talk, but her voice was no longer audible to Jarek. Her mouth was moving, but Jarek could not understand what she was saying to the young man for a few moments. Then Sarah's voice resurfaced again as suddenly as it had disappeared.

"I assume you are bound to this house, as to never lose you. I just don't fully understand what the purpose is."

"I can't stay here. The creature here is determined to trap me here forever. To control me somehow. I can feel myself growing weaker and weaker each day."

"Can you describe it to me, Samuel? The creature that is after you. What are you feeling while you are here? Anything you can share might assist me in helping you."

The spirit remained quiet, giving Sarah no recognition of the questions she asked it.

"I am sorry, Samuel. I just need more information to try and help you."

The silence was nearly deafening. Then the spirit's mouth opened.

"I feel as though I am standing at the bottom of a great chasm, all alone. I am standing here, crying out for help, but no one ever answers back. Feeling lost, hopeless. I fear no one is able to hear me or help me. Yet I can hear others yelling into the chasm searching for me, a whirlwind of voices and echoes, but neither whoever is yelling nor myself seems to truly be able to hear each other and make contact. I try climbing out of the chasm with no success. I try harder, but it only results in my fingertips being bloodied, leaving faint bloody finger trails all around on the rocky walls. I am trapped, there is no escape."

Sarah stood still with no response. Trying to consume what the spirit just told her. After a moment, she took a deep breath.

"It is exactly what I thought, Samuel. The attempt was to permanently bind you here. But I don't believe it is because of the fear of losing you and always wanting you close. I believe it is to trap you here for the true monster. For you to feed an inhuman spirit so that its power may be used," Sarah said bluntly and with great worry in her voice.

"I fear that to be true, too," the young man responded with a shaking voice.

The room began to grow even darker. A heavy feeling began to fall on Jarek. He suddenly couldn't catch his breath. The hair on his arms and neck stood straight up. The ghost of Samuel looked toward the corner where the hidden door in the bookcase was.

"Samuel, Samuel, what is it?" asked Sarah worriedly.

"Sarah, you must go. It's coming," he responded with eyes wide and filled with worry.

"What is it, Samuel? Who is it? If I know who it is, I'll be able to help release you to move on!"

"Sarah, go!" exclaimed the boy.

Sarah turned and ran toward the door leading to the hallway. The room grew unbearably dark and heavy. It was like standing on the edge of marsh on a humid, foggy, cloud-covered night when not even the glow of the moon was able to penetrate through the clouds.

As Sarah was about to reach for the doorknob to open the already slightly open door, it slammed shut. She frantically tried to pull open the door, but it didn't budge. The air in the room began to swirl, and the drapes began to blow as if the windows were wide open during a storm. Jarek looked, and the windows were tightly sealed. Books fell from the shelves. The lamps began flickering so much it caused several of the bulbs to burst with the energy surges.

Sarah turned from the door, looking back into the room with absolute terror. The rug that Jarek had looked at earlier flew back as if someone had pulled it with all their strength. A great force knocked the furniture away that had been sitting on it.

Jarek's eyes narrowed.

There, burnt into the hardwood was a massive seal filled with symbols. It was exactly what Jarek had feared. It wasn't one of the protection or charm seals he had noted in the book. It was a demon's seal. A seal one would use to conjure the entity from the depths of hell. Jarek could clearly see the circle of symbols, at least ten feet wide. A pentagram in the center, and various markings that correlated with whatever demon was brought into this world. Jarek began to quickly take mental notes of the symbols surrounding the pentagram.

Jarek's concentration on the seal was quickly broken when Sarah let out a blood-curdling scream. His eyes refocused on the center of the room as a figure made entirely of black mist began to appear. Jarek watched in horror as Samuel's ghost began to be restrained and wrapped in chains. The skin on the boy began to grow pale and gray, as if decomposing right before Jarek's eyes.

The boy's ghost turned toward Jarek . . . While looking directly at him, stitches began to pierce the boy's lips. One stitch at time, slowly . . . methodically. The boy could no longer speak. The room grew louder and louder as the air continued to swirl.

"Samuel! No!" Sarah shouted as she ran toward the now chain-bound spirit.

Right as Sarah appeared to touch the spirit, her arm went right through it as he faded away. Instead, she ran right into Jarek and stopped, taking a gasp of air.

Jarek stood shocked. Had he somehow transported into this moment in time, he wondered. He quickly realized no, he hadn't.

Jarek gazed into Sarah's eyes as her life force began to fade. Blood began to drip from her mouth. He slowly broke his stare and began to look down. An arm, a man's arm, passed through Jarek's transparent body just as Sarah had run through Samuel's ghost.

Jarek's eyes looked down the man's arm to the wrist, then to the hand. The hand was grasping the handle of a knife. The blade that followed was resting inside the chest of Sarah. The hand began to slowly move the knife in and out . . . butchering . . . in and out. The man was working his way around her heart. Her body appeared to be held by the dark mist filling the room.

On the last stroke of the knife, the man pulled out the blade. With his other arm, he once again passed through Jarek, reaching directly into Sarah's gaping chest and retrieved her heart.

Jarek saw the light of Sarah's eyes vanish in an instant. Her lifeless body finally fell to the ground.

The room became calm. Still black as night but calm. The man's hand holding the dead woman's heart. Then he threw it in the air. Jarek watched as the bloody heart landed directly in the center of the seal.

The tissue of the organ began to grow black, like a smoldering log at the bottom of a fire. The smoldering quickly turned to ash. Then the heart simply was absorbed into the seal, as if it had never been there. Jarek began to turn slowly to see the face that belonged to the man who had thrown the heart.

"Mr. Videni! Mr. Videni! Are you alright?"

Jarek's eyes refocused as if he had just awoken from a deep sleep. He was standing at the base of the stairs, just where he had been in his vision.

"Jarek, dinner is ready and waiting," continued the voice sternly.

Jarek blinked several times and looked toward the doorway. His eyes were mostly refocused in the present, yet pieces of the vision seemed to be lingering. He continued to blink. Jarek's eyes were finally able to see who was talking. In the hall, just past the library door, stood Martin peering in.

"Jarek!" Martin finally shouted.

"Yes, sorry! I must have been . . . I must have been sleepwalking," Jarek responded, with a tone of unease.

Jarek could clearly see Martin, but everything around him was hazy, dark, and shadowy.

"Well, it happens to everyone," Martin said quickly. "Come along, it's time for dinner. It's already nearly nine p.m. after all."

"I'll . . . I'll follow you down."

Martin turned and began to walk downstairs to the dining room. The dark haze turned simultaneously with his body. However, the dark haze floated away in the opposite direction that Martin began to walk. Jarek took the long way toward the door. Looking back, he noticed the book he had been looking through was now sitting on the side table by one of the chairs. He must have set it down while experiencing the vision. He walked over where the massive burnt seal was in his vision, under the Persian carpet. Using the toe of his boot, he gently lifted the opposite corner of the carpet he had previously moved. There were remnants of something, something someone had clearly tried to oil out of the wood.

"Mr. Videni!" Martin shouted from the end of the hallway.

"Yes, sir, on my way," Jarek replied as he hustled out of the library and caught up with Martin at the top of the stairs.

"Thought I lost you again," Martin said with a slight grin before venturing down the stairs.

Ж

Jarek took the last bite of Beef Wellington as everyone sat in silence during the meal. The whole while, Jarek could tell that Martin and

Annie were not in a conversational mood. The darkness he had witnessed during his vision still kept his hair standing on end. Though Jarek could not see the force since being in the library, he certainly continued to feel its energy surrounding him now throughout the entirety of this home.

"Well that certainly was delicious!" Jarek said as Rose walked into the dining room to clear the dishes.

Even though Jarek made the statement to help break the silence, he said it toward Rose because she likely cooked most of the food anyway. Rose gave him a nod of acknowledgment as she stacked several dishes and brought them back toward the kitchen.

"Yes, it was very delicious," Annie stated as she perked up slightly.

"That's right, it's your favorite," Jarek responded. "I haven't had it to eat in a very long time."

"Well, Rose is kind enough to make sure we have it at least once a month for me."

"Yes, Rose certainly takes good care of us," Martin said, interjecting himself into the conversation.

"That is a fine thing to find these days. Someone who cares, and goes out of their way to ensure people are looked after," said Jarek.

"Yes. It certainly is," Annie said with slight attitude as her eyes shifted toward Martin for a moment.

Jarek felt as if another argument between them was about to begin.

"Well, again, thank you so much. However, I think I should retire for the night. I need some rest tonight," Jarek stated before any conflict between Martin and Annie could erupt.

"Yes, I think that is an excellent idea," Martin responded quickly.

"We all need a good night's sleep, I believe," Annie said with raised brows as she stood from her seat.

Martin and Jarek rose from their places as well. Annie began to walk out of the room.

"Have a good night, Miss Annie."

"You too, Mr. Videni," Annie said as she clearly looked at her father, paused, then turned and walked away.

"I am sorry about that, Jarek," Martin said quietly with a look of embarrassment.

"Oh, no need to apologize, Martin. What you all are going through is bound . . ." Jarek took a long pause. "What you all are going through is sure to cause frustration and conflict. It is all so much to deal with."

"Thank you for understanding, Jarek."

"Certainly," Jarek responded while nodding his head. "Have yourself a good night," he continued as he reached over and shook Martin's hand.

"You as well." Martin reached back and gave a light and quick handshake.

Jarek turned and headed up to his room. He removed his clothing and washed his face and hands. Jarek then lit a small fire in the fireplace to keep his room a bit warmer before falling asleep. He looked around the room; everything seemed calm and felt comfortable. As he crawled into the bed, the blankets were chilly but quickly warmed from his body heat.

Jarek looked at the clock on the mantel above the fireplace. The time was 11:34 p.m. There was an oddly pure calmness in the home. Certainly, a stark contrast to what he had experienced only several hours ago. Jarek's stomach was still satisfied with his dinner of Beef Wellington. He looked at the bite mark on his wrist, which seemed to be subsiding. He was looking forward to a full night's rest, knowing that tomorrow would be another day. One that he hoped deep inside might bring more answers. A day that would bring him closer to discovering what actually happened, how Samuel had been bound to this house, and who cut out Sarah O'Connell's heart.

CHAPTER 8

THE CEMETERY

December 22, 1924, 8:19 a.m.

The sun beamed through the tall windows of Jarek's bedroom. It filled the room with a bright shimmer from the light bouncing off the snow outside, rushing through the glass of the windows, and then reflecting off the small crystal chandelier hanging from the ceiling above the bed. After a restful night of sleep, Jarek slowly opened his eyes to the morning light flooding the room. He continued to lay there for a few moments simply enjoying the great night of rest, the elegance of the room he was staying in, and the warmth of being under the quilts. He knew that once he crawled out from under the covers, the room would feel chilly. Even though there was a radiator in the room, the fireplace had gone out overnight, and being such a large room, it still felt cold in the mornings. Jarek moved his eyes up toward his bedside table to look at the time: 8:25 a.m. *I better get up for the day and get ready*, he thought to himself. After everything that transpired yesterday, he had some research to do.

As soon as he moved the quilts to crawl out of bed, Jarek almost regretted it, because the chill of the room quickly rushed over his arms, chest, and legs, giving him goose bumps. He moved to the fireplace and placed some kindling and a few logs on the still smoldering embers. A small flame ignited in the kindling, which soon lit the logs. The fire gave off just enough heat for Jarek to feel a little better as it warmed his body slightly. He turned and walked to the bathroom to shave and get ready for the day. He still was reveling in having his own private bathroom. In New York, Jarek lived in a boarding house for bachelors and had to share the lavatory with three other men who lived in the home.

Once he finished getting clean, he walked to the closet and retrieved his clothes for the day. As he began to get dressed, he noticed another slip of paper folded on the small table where he had done his tarot reading and the note with the name of Dr. Monroe. Someone had come into the room while he was getting ready in the bathroom. The thought of the intrusion sent a shiver down his spine.

Jarek moved toward the table and grabbed the note. He gently unfolded it to reveal the writing on it. It was the same handwriting as the first letter he received and the note with Martin's doctor, Dr. Monroe's name. This note was nearly as short as the last and simply read, *Oakland Cemetery ~ Front Street*.

Rushing back to the bathroom, Jarek quickly made sure his hair was oiled and combed. He went out into his room, put his suit coat on, laced his boots up, and walked briskly from his room and down to the main level. The whole time, he was trying to determine who the author of the letters and the notes could be. He had an inkling but no evidence to verify.

The foyer was empty, so Jarek glanced into the dining room. It too was empty. So, he moved across the foyer to the parlor. No one was in there either. When he backed away from the parlor archway, he noticed a door to the right that he didn't see on the tour when he had first arrived. He was too curious of a person not to look. Jarek reached out to grab hold of the glass doorknob.

"Mr. Videni."

"Yes," he responded as he turned to see Rose standing in the foyer. "Well, good morning Ms. Smith."

"Good morning, sir. We have your breakfast still warm in the kitchen. If you'd like to eat, that is?"

"Yes, I was just thinking some breakfast would do me good."

"Wonderful—follow me, please," she said as she turned to walk toward the kitchen. "We weren't entirely sure if you were hungry since you slept fairly late today."

"I'm sorry about that. I must have needed the rest."

"Quite all right, sir. Lucky for you, we have a pot of coffee on the stove. It will help to wake you for the day ahead."

Jarek was almost caught off guard; Rose had the hint of a smile and an unusual pleasantness about herself this morning.

"Ms. Smith, what room is that through the door there?" Jarek asked, gesturing toward the room he was just about to walk into.

"Oh, that door? That just goes into Mr. O'Connell's study. He is in there working right now. He spends many hours in there some days. Not as many hours as Annie spends in the library, but still a significant amount of time. I think he likes having the office space here. When he goes down to the printing shop, I believe he gets too distracted to get any paperwork done."

"I am sure he is appreciative of it."

As they both walked into the kitchen, Jarek could smell coffee and the remnant smells of breakfast. Rose walked over to the small table off to the side of the kitchen and uncovered a plate of eggs, bacon, and well-done toast.

"Mr. Videni, please sit here," Rose said while gesturing to the seat with the plate of food in front of it. "I will pour you a cup of coffee. Do you take cream or sugar?" she asked.

"No, thank you, I drink it black," he responded while taking the seat at the table. "This looks fantastic. Thank you so much for keeping some food for me."

"No trouble at all. As I said, Mr. O'Connell is in the study today. I'm sure he will be fairly busy all day, too. He tries to work ahead so that he is able to enjoy the holidays here at home. Miss Annie is upstairs in the library reading, I believe, and later she is heading downtown to get her final fitting on her dress for the Christmas Eve party. I will be running errands most of the day as well, in preparation for the party. So, if you need anything today, you will have to simply help yourself."

"Oh, that is very fine with me. I have a few items I want to take care of as well," Jarek responded.

Jarek knew that as soon as he finished breakfast, he wanted to find out where Oakland Cemetery was.

"Wonderful. Oh, and Mr. O'Connell handed me one of his nicer suits to leave in your room to try on for the party. He said there is no need for you to spend money on a new one. You both seem to be about the same size anyway. I will just set it out on your bed."

"Thank you, Ms. Smith. I really appreciate it."

"Miss Annie will be selecting her mask for the evening once she gets her final fitting today as well. I will ask her to purchase one for you, too. Unless of course you brought your own?" Rose asked sarcastically and with a smile.

"A mask?" Jarek asked.

"Well, of course. You can't very well attend a masquerade without a mask, sir," Rose said as she secured her list of errands sitting on the table by him and then walked out of the kitchen while putting on a long black coat and emerald-green hat, leaving Jarek to eat his breakfast alone.

Jarek finished eating while perusing the pages of *The Saint Paul Dispatch*. He helped himself to a second cup of coffee as he finished reading some of the printed local stories. While he finished cleaning up his breakfast mess, Jarek was trying to deduce the best way to find out information on Oakland Cemetery. Suddenly, it dawned on him. While he was sitting in the parlor on the first night he arrived, he had seen a framed map of Saint Paul hanging on the wall. He rushed toward the parlor, being sure to be quiet while walking across the foyer so that Martin would not hear his footsteps from the study.

Once Jarek crossed through the archway, he stopped. There on the wall hung the entire layout of Saint Paul. He hadn't realized just how large the city really was until he was able to see it in its entirety.

Jarek moved closer to the framed map. He quickly was able to find SPUD; then he found the state capitol building's location. He knew the cathedral was not too far from there because of his walk to Dr. Monroe's office. Once he found the cathedral, it was easy to find Saint Claire Street and the O'Connell mansion. He continued to scan the map.

"Aha, there you are," he whispered quietly to himself. On the north end, past the state capitol a little way, was Oakland Cemetery. He took mental note of the best route to get there from the mansion.

The sheer size of the cemetery was impressive to Jarek. It appeared to be a fairly long walk to the massive cemetery . . . and he still did not know exactly what to expect once he got there. He thought to himself that he was going in even more blind to this situation than compared to when he came to the O'Connell mansion initially. Jarek did not have a single inkling of what to expect. But he knew that someone wanted him there, and he thought it might be someone who had answers to the many questions circulating in his mind.

Jarek went back upstairs to his room, securing his coat and hat to stay warm while making the walk to the cemetery. Thankfully, it didn't look too cold outside, and there were snow flurries gently falling to the ground as to indicate no chilly wind. He double-checked his boots to ensure they were tied tight. He noticed Martin's suit laid out on the bed but knew he didn't have time to try it on now, so he headed down to the kitchen to exit out the back door of the home, hoping he would remain inconspicuous to make his venture to the cemetery.

⚸

While walking for about forty minutes, Jarek passed the Cathedral of Saint Paul, the state capitol building, and finally he was beginning to pass part of the Oakland Cemetery as he headed toward what appeared to be the main entrance along Front Street. Jarek walked through the entrance. A sign was posted off to the side of the drive: NO AUTOMOBILES BEYOND THIS POINT. Within just his first few steps, he immediately began to admire his surroundings. The grounds were fairly wooded with tall bare oak trees. Mausoleums and headstones dotted the rolling rolls. Everything slightly covered in snow was truly beautiful.

Jarek still did not know who or what he was specifically looking for. He figured the best choice would be to simply walk around the grounds. He didn't mind that approach either. Jarek enjoyed walking through cemeteries . . . for several reasons. He had had many experiences of all types in graveyards, from exciting encounters with entities to calming and meaningful moments that he would always treasure.

Continuing down the path, Jarek began reading the names on the headstones of the people buried there, dating back to the Civil War era. There were monuments and headstones of all types, from simple memorials in the ground to grand tombs and statues. He felt the most peaceful that he had since leaving New York City and coming to Saint Paul. This peacefulness allowed for him to truly think and process everything that had occurred since he arrived on the train to this city.

The path seemed to go on for a way, with several forks and side paths to choose from. Jarek began to hear a gentle flow of water from the creek, just ever so slightly. It was most likely nearly frozen over, he thought to himself. Sure enough, after he walked around a small bend in the path and up a small hill, he came to a bridge over a creek. A gently flowing creek that was mostly iced over wound its way through the cemetery. The sound of the water flowing, birds singing and chirping, and the distant rumble of automobiles muffled by the snow coverage was all Jarek could hear. The grounds of cemetery were vacant . . . except for one person he could see standing near a headstone in the distance.

As Jarek crossed the small stone bridge, he continued to admire the cemetery grounds and the beauty of nature in the middle of a bustling city. If he hadn't walked here during the daylight, he would have sworn he had left the city entirely. As he continued to walk, he was getting closer to the only other person he could see. It became clear it was a woman in a long black coat, an emerald-green hat, and a sable-colored muff over her hands. He knew this combination looked familiar from just this morning. She was standing near a small gray granite headstone. Jarek could tell that she was deep in thought and unaware that someone was approaching her.

"Good morning, Ms. Smith," Jarek said in a tone as to not startle her.

She made a slight jump as she turned to see who was talking to her.

"Oh, good morning, Mr. Videni," she responded. "I was lost in thought there for a moment."

"No worries. I did not mean to startle you. But I also did not want to appear to be lurking," Jarek responded with a small grin.

Rose gave a small smile back.

"I wouldn't have assumed that, Mr. Videni. I was wondering if you had even found my note this morning and were able to find where Oakland Cemetery was located. Your deduction and resourcefulness skills are on point."

"Thank you . . ." Jarek slowly responded, glad that his intuition of who the author was, was in fact correct. "To be honest, I wasn't entirely positive that you were the one to reach out for my assistance. However, there was a few subtle clues that it was you along the way."

"I figured between leaving the list of my day's activities to see my handwriting, and hoping you'd remember that when you first arrived I placed you in the parlor . . . in a chair that looks directly at the map of the city."

"That was very clever, Ms. Smith. But why all the charades?"

"Isn't it obvious? It's not safe to talk in the house. I can't have them knowing what you are really doing here. Especially if Sarah's killer is still in the house. I knew you would be able to look at this situation from an entirely new perspective than I have . . . and a perspective the local authority would never be able to."

"Do you really believe that Sarah's killer is Martin or Annie?" Jarek asked with a bit of hesitation and doubt in his voice.

"Well, yes and no. I know you have felt and seen that there is something dark within the O'Connell home. Something isn't right, and I knew you would be able to help me."

"How did you know though? How did you know to reach out to me, or even who I am for that matter?"

"That, Jarek, is a story for another time," Rose stated, calling him by his first name finally.

"But how . . ." Jarek began to ask as Rose cut him off.

"Jarek, there is a more urgent matter at hand. I already told you the story about the night that Sarah was murdered, but now I must tell you the full story, starting back at the beginning. I could not share all these details with you in the home, for I didn't know who, or what, was listening to us in the library."

Chasing Shadows ~ Genesis

As Rose was talking, Jarek's eyes began to drift toward the headstone that she was standing by:

Samuel David Smith
Beloved Son, Brother, and Friend
November 16, 1906 – May 16, 1924

"He is my son," she said. Rose then gestured to a very small headstone right next to the one for Samuel:

James Samuel Smith
Though you never walked in this life, may you now walk in paradise.
June 5, 1896

"James was my first child. He's the reason I ended up working for the O'Connell family. I was unwed and with child, and the family took me in. Martin's parents, that is. Unfortunately, when I was ready to give birth, I knew something wasn't right. My boy was born already gone from this world."

Rose took a deep breath. "I never got to truly meet him, but I miss him every day."

"Losing someone is never easy."

"Anyway, I continued to work for the family. They treated me so kind and were so caring. I loved working for them. I continued to work for them for nearly ten more years. In the beginning of 1906, I met a man. His name was David. He was working temporarily at the printing factory as he was passing through town on his way out west. He had intended to work for only a few days in Saint Paul to earn more money to finish his journey to California. But he and I began to spend a lot of time together. He knew just how to charm me and make me feel so important. David shared with me his life story.

"Within a few months we discovered I was with child again. We were both nervous and excited. Of course, we knew society would be judgmental, but neither of us were ready to get married either. The O'Connells did let him move into the home. He spent his time at the factory and helping repair things in their home. I gave birth to Samuel during the first snowfall of the season. He was a beautiful, healthy baby. David seemed to adore him and never left our side those first few days. I expected that he and I were going to get married and start our family together.

"However, on Christmas morning, I woke up and realized my expectations were not going to be met. David had packed up his few belongings and had left in the night. I have never heard from him again. I was in shock and disbelief, but the O'Connells were there for me and assured me that I . . . that Samuel and I always had a place in their family."

Rose brushed a tear that began to roll down her cheek.

"I am sure you had such a mix of emotions during this time," Jarek said. "I am so sorry you had to go through this."

"All of what I have gone through I believe has made me stronger as a person." Rose cleared her throat. "Anyway, during this same time when David had left, Martin took over responsibility of the printing factory, and he was nearing completion of the mansion. He asked me to come and work for him. I hated to leave the O'Connells in their house up on Summit Avenue, but alas, they did pass away from illness early that spring in 1907.

"Since Martin had just finished building and moving into his own home with Sarah, he sold his parent's house on Summit Avenue to a man who owned a division of the railroad. We then moved into the new home with Martin and Sarah by summer. Sarah had just given birth to Annie, so the home felt so busy. It was a new home that everyone was getting settled into, training the new staff, and raising two young ones. But it was exciting, and I wouldn't change it for the world."

Rose took a long pause. "I'm sorry, should we walk? I just realized I am little chilly standing here."

"Absolutely. I don't mind walking one bit," Jarek replied.

"Excellent," Rose said as she turned, and they began to continue down the path through cemetery. "Well, as the years progressed, Samuel and Annie became really good friends. Martin became more prominent in the community, taking on the role that his father had. So, they began to fulfill his dream of hosting grand parties. Sarah spent her days volunteering in the community, helping both children with their school studies, playing piano herself and teaching Samuel, too. She also was a spiritualist, so would spend lots of time with her friends from the community discussing and studying her gifts in the library."

"Studying her gifts?" Jarek asked.

"Yes, Sarah believed she was a medium and would host gatherings with other members of the community. She would often spend evenings researching new ways to help communicate with those already passed on in case they may have messages for loved ones. Some people mock her, but she touched many lives in this city while using her talents."

While stopping midstride, Rose turned toward Jarek. "I tell you this in confidence, Mr. Videni. I tell you because I know that you do have an open mind and that you yourself know that there is so much more to this world than what meets the eye."

"Of course, Ms. Smith. You can trust me," he responded as they resumed walking.

"Well, you see, the troubles in the O'Connell house really didn't arrive until this year. It is as if the house now somehow has an unwanted guest that is nothing but an insidious dark being."

"How do you mean?"

"My son Samuel was always a little different while growing up. I believe this is why Sarah took such a liking to him. He would talk about his dreams and conversations with people that had already passed on. He would claim to see beings all around, beings that none of us could see. Sarah and he shared a bond over their unique connection to the peculiar. However, sometimes at school, he would be mocked for being so different. Or he was oftentimes accused of lying. So he began to not talk about the experiences anymore. He put his focus entirely into the piano and his schoolwork. He developed a stronger relationship with Annie during this time too. They were inseparable at times."

Jarek continued to listen to Rose as he was trying to piece together everyone's perspectives of Samuel, the poor young man bound to the O'Connell home. His mind kept returning to the vision he had seen of the young man in the library.

"Mind you, it was not a romantic relationship. Strictly platonic. He struggled with other people outside of the home, but it was all still so beautiful. It seemed like we were all one family . . ." Rose drifted off, and it was clear to Jarek that her thoughts had begun to retreat inside her mind.

"We can take a break if you would like."

"No . . . No, I need to tell you. This might be our only opportunity. Samuel was such a good son. He always followed the rules. He always respected those older than him or in authority over him. In fact, I'll never forget that anytime he was serving dinner, he would always place the meals in front of people in order of age instead of serving the ladies first. A little uncommon, but it was how he thought it should be, so the O'Connells always allowed it and never corrected him."

Rose chuckled very slightly to herself, clearly having wonderful thoughts while thinking back on when Samuel was still alive.

"Well, the occurrences this year seemed to all happen so fast. It was in May that Samuel began to share a lot more about his gifts again. It had been so long that it did seem unusual, but he also was much happier talking about it again. And then one day, my world came to a halt."

Rose slowed her pace and stopped talking. She crossed to the other side of the path to an iron bench. She brushed away some powdery snow and then sat down. She then brushed more snow off and patted the bench seat, indicating for Jarek to take a seat. He sat down, placing one arm on his own lap and resting the other along the back of the bench.

"Samuel had been downtown all day, spending time with another boy from the school that he went to. He would go fishing or walk in the park with him, even during the summer when school wasn't in session. Samuel came home that evening very distraught, and he clearly had been crying. I do not know what it was about, and when I tried to confront him, he only told me to mind my own business, that he was eighteen years old and could handle his own issues. I know that this other boy had mocked Samuel in the past when he shared details about his gifts with him. I can only assume that this had been brought up again and that the young man had been cruel to him once again."

Rose drifted off a bit once more. She took a deep breath.

"Well, the next morning when I went to awaken Samuel, I knocked on the door. He didn't respond. I . . . I opened the door to his room, and that's when I found him."

Rose removed her hands from her fur muff and wiped away tears in both eyes. "I found that he had hung himself during the night from the rafter in his room."

"I am so sorry, Rose," Jarek said as he moved his arm from the back of the bench down onto Rose's shoulders.

"Well, it was a shock to me and the entire family. Obviously, I had much difficulty dealing with it. I think Annie had an extremely hard time with it, too. Ever since Samuel's death she has devoted her entire time to her studies in the library. She is placing all of her passion and energy into learning as much as she can . . . about anything. She is extremely smart. It is extraordinary and might be some good that has come out of his death."

"That is encouraging. As long as she has not become a total recluse. She has had much to deal with, so I am sure she is handling it the best she can."

"Exactly. I would not want to pressure her on how best to handle grief." Rose straightened her back. "Jarek, did you have an opportunity to meet with Dr. Monroe?"

"Yes, I went to his office downtown yesterday. We had a very . . . enlightening conversation."

"I'm glad. I hope it showed you just more of the oddities that have begun occurring in the household since Samuel's passing."

"Yes. Granted, I'll admit, since arriving here I just continue to generate more questions than find answers. Do you believe the doctor's assessment of Martin?"

"I have known Martin now for over eighteen years. He is a good man, and he has a good heart. I cannot see him ever doing anything to hurt someone. Yet I can tell you that I did witness an evening in April when he, Sarah, and a few friends tried to contact the other side in an attempt to find Martin some answers to some issues he had been dealing with. However, that night just created more questions. That is, until he met with Dr. Monroe, and I heard firsthand what his assessment was. I can say I have never seen Martin act in the ways that he has over these past few months.

"If I judged him solely on what I have witnessed over these past few months, I would agree more with what Annie believes, and it would justify her being scared of him. Yet in my heart and knowing him, I would agree with Dr. Monroe. Martin clearly has demons from his past that he needs to work through, but I do not believe that this trauma has led him to being a malevolent person now. However, Annie is his daughter, and she has a connection with him that is currently being strained by something."

"I am glad you say that. I need to hear outside perspectives."

"What do you feel and see when you're talking to Martin?"

"I would agree personally more so with Dr. Monroe. I do feel that something is wrong with Martin, and he is dealing with something internally, but I believe it is mental and not spiritual. I do not feel anything dark within him, nor do I see anything dark . . . but I have been fooled before," Jarek said, thinking about not only past experiences but also remembering seeing The Magician card only two nights ago during the Tarot reading.

"So how do we move forward with helping them?"

"Well, honestly, I believe it might be time to try and make communication with whatever may be in the house. It might be our only way to find some answers to at least a few of our questions."

Rose turned her head, looking out toward the cemetery. "I was afraid you were going to say that."

"Have you ever been a part of a séance?" Jarek asked her.

"I have on a few occasions. Like I said, Mrs. O'Connell was a medium. She would have guests over from her spiritual circle several times throughout the year. Typically, it would be around a solstice or equinox. They would either just have a party or sometimes do Tarot readings, but sometimes they would hold a séance. I would partake sometimes if they needed an additional person. The last one we did was this past June. The twenty-first of June, the summer solstice."

She paused, then placed her face into her hands.

"Was it an attempt to reach Samuel?" Jarek asked, already knowing the answer.

"Yes. I just . . . We all just wanted to know why he chose to leave us."

"Did you have any success reaching him?"

"Sarah claims to have made a little contact but did not disclose any of the conversation. The rest of us, Annie, and myself, only heard knocking as a response and witnessed a few items move slightly throughout the room. I did have a moment where it did feel like he was in the room, simply as a presence. Oh! And I swear I could smell the scent of the aftershave he would use. I remember thinking at one point, though I can't see him, I still felt I could reach out and run my fingers through his long hair."

"That is similar to many people's experiences who are not gifted with mediumship. In fact, every medium is different in their abilities, I have discovered."

"Well, it was a positive experience at first. But then Sarah said she couldn't talk with him. Like someone was restraining him or muffling him, or that it really wasn't Samuel. The room got a heavy feeling. Then it went dark, not that the candles went out, but like a shadow just filled the room. Full of hopelessness. The feeling and smell of Samuel was gone, and then abruptly it all went away. Sarah said the connection had broken, but I believe she broke it in order to stop whatever it was trying to stop Samuel from contacting us."

"That can be a difficult position to be in. I have seen too many dark beings throughout my life that would take advantage of destroying anything that has a spark of hope in it."

"I would very much like to try again. Every so often, when I am cleaning the house or simply reading a book, I still get a feeling that Samuel is nearby. But I do still wish I knew why he did what he did." Rose paused. "Maybe by finding answers to Sarah's death, we will find answers to his."

"I would be honored to assist with finding those answers and help bring closure. I do believe you in feeling Samuel. I, too, have seen a presence, several in fact. I believe that Samuel is in the house."

"Really?" Rose asked with a glee of hope in her voice.

"Remember, I said maybe. My visions and interactions with those who have gone from our world or other entities is all different. Sometimes it is hard for me to decipher contact from individuals."

"Oh, I would be so grateful if you were able to help."

"I will do what I can. That's all I can promise."

"Thank you, Jarek. You are a good man," Rose said as she stood, implying that she was ready to leave.

"Thank you, Ms. Smith," Jarek responded as he stood.

They started to move down the path back in the direction they came from.

"Please, Jarek, call me Rose when we are together. No need to be formal outside of the home."

He knew immediately that she meant to remain formal in the house. This would allow for less likelihood of someone knowing they were working together on this journey.

"Also, I am sorry for having you meet me in the cemetery. It is the only location I knew of that would be the most private for us to talk. I am assuming cemeteries are difficult for you to be in?"

"Oh, friends of mine have often thought that. But to be truthful, I greatly enjoy being in a cemetery. It is a great place to think and ponder."

"I meant as it relates to the dead," Rose interjected. "You must see some terrible things in cemeteries, and to feel so much grief at one time."

"Oh, on the contrary. I believe places like this are a beautiful thing. Grief is a difficult and odd feeling for everyone. Each of us experiences grief in a different way. But it is a part of life that every person must go through. There can be grief from losing a beloved animal, grief from someone dying, or even grief from someone abandoning another person for other opportunities. Being able to feel that grief can be overwhelming for me at times, but it helps me stay grounded in why I do what I do. It keeps the humanity at the forefront for me when dealing with too many dark things."

Jarek turned out, looking over the cemetery grounds, as if seeing it again for the first time.

"Being here is where I can find purpose for my gifts. Picture it this way: a beautiful bustling train station with many tracks going all directions. There are several different platforms, many trains coming and going. There are people by themselves, there are families, and there are groups of friends. The people are sad to be saying goodbye, yet for those arriving, it is a joyful reunion. That is what being in a cemetery is like for me. Sure, it can be sad saying goodbye to your loved ones getting on a train to go somewhere else, but it is someone getting on a train to go on their next journey, to move on to the next chapter in their life. That is also comforting. And sometimes it might be someone arriving by train to visit for a short time just to say hello to loved ones.

"That is the beauty of it for me. It is a place where people can reunite or where people move on and take their next step down life's road. Once in a while, I get to help someone find the right train platform for them to take that next step. It is a mix of joy and sadness. But it all has a silver lining of hope, because we all know that one day, we will all meet again. I get to see that, and I get to feel that each time I'm in a place like this. So don't apologize to me, Rose. I should be thanking you for bringing me here."

They had reached the entrance to the cemetery and were standing near the No Automobiles beyond This Point sign.

"You're welcome Jarek," Rose said with a smile and a few tears still rolling down her cheeks. "Well, you better head back to the house. I will return there after a while. I need to meet Annie downtown to make sure she got her dress fitted, and after that, she and I will find you that mask!"

CHAPTER 9

The Magician

December 23, 1924, 5:35 p.m.

Jarek sat in the loft of the library in one of the high-back chairs. He had taken his time getting back to the O'Connell home after the cemetery. He took that time to ponder and analyze the information he had obtained since arriving in Saint Paul. Once he was inside the house, he continued with his thoughts while simultaneously formulating his plan for this evening's event as he sat there in the loft. Jarek was unsure of what manner he should try to contact the beings in the house. He knew that he still needed to learn how to unlock his full potential and abilities. He had contacted the dead several times, but he knew deep inside that he could create a stronger connection and have a further reach to those who have passed on.

So far, Jarek had found that simple meditation worked to make nominal contact if the spirit hadn't moved on. However, he knew that the best way to make a stronger connection was by being the medium to a full séance with multiple people. This additional energy increased the likelihood of being able to reach further into the veil. In Jarek's experience, a séance of three to six people had the best results. Having less than three created so little energy that it was hard for him to help those on the other side make contact. However, having more than six people led to too much energy and caused confusion in the communication with spirits.

Jarek was so deep in thought while sitting in the chair that he hadn't noticed the library door slowly opening down below. He didn't notice the figure stepping across the threshold and moving toward the base of the staircase.

"What are you doing up there?" said a loud voice from a man.

"Oh, Martin, sorry. I didn't see you come in," responded Jarek, clearly startled.

"Quit calling me that! I told you my name is Peter," he responded angrily.

"I'm sorry . . ." Jarek hesitated. "P-Peter . . . I didn't see you come in."

"We aren't supposed to be in here. Nobody is supposed to touch her belongings."

"Whose belongings, Peter?"

"Don't be stupid. The lady of the house, of course."

"Why aren't we supposed to touch them though?"

"It doesn't like them moved. It wants them left right where she had left them before . . . Well, before you know what."

"But doesn't Annie come in here often to read?" Jarek asked him, trying to figure out what "Peter" meant by his statements.

"No! What don't you understand? Even Annie knows not to touch these things without permission. They need to stay exactly where they were, or else it gets very angry. So get down here, and leave her stuff alone."

"All right, all right. I'm coming down."

"Thank you. I don't like when it gets angry. It's its house after all. These are the rules we need to follow."

Jarek began to descend down the staircase toward Martin very slowly, as he was still trying to figure out the best approach to continue this conversation with Martin's second consciousness, the boy named Peter.

"Are there many rules for you to follow, or just to not touch Mrs. O'Connell's belongings?" Jarek asked.

"Not many, as long as I never disturb anything or anyone. It's pretty easy to follow the rules. Besides, you break them once, and you will always remember to not do it again!"

"Why's that? What happens when you break the rules?"

"You get locked away for a very long time. You aren't allowed to do anything. You can't eat, sleep, or even taste food . . . You're locked away in a dark place. It is very horrible . . ."

The man that thought he was a boy got very glum and his gaze seemed to drift into blackness. He opened his mouth. "No . . . no. It is just best to do what you are supposed to and simply follow the rules," he said while shaking his head in agreement with his own statement.

"That sounds horrible. I see why it is best to just do as you're told," Jarek stated.

"Yes, it certainly is. Anyway, sir, it is time to eat dinner. I can smell the food!" the boy said as he turned and began to run out of the library like a child rushing downstairs on Christmas morning to open gifts.

"I'm right behind you," Jarek said.

"Perfect. I will let them know," he responded as he stopped just outside the door and turned his head back toward Jarek. "Oh, and sir . . ."

"Yes?" Jarek asked.

"Always follow the rules. Not worth risking it, you will be caught."

"Is it easy to be caught?"

"You are such a goof. Of course it is easy to be caught when it is always watching you."

The boy turned and ran down the hall, leaving Jarek sanding still as a shiver went up his body.

Ж

Jarek slowly made his way from the library. Ever since leaving the library and continuing as he crossed the foyer, Jarek felt as if he were once again being watched. He didn't know if it was the dark presence he had felt and seen multiple times now, or if it was simply his imagination running wild since his interaction with Martin upstairs.

The smell of pork, boiled potatoes, and buttery fresh-baked bread wafted through the house. The delicious smells made Jarek's stomach ache for food. It also made him realize he had not eaten anything since breakfast.

As Jarek got closer to the dining room, he could hear the workers placing the last bit of the table settings and platters of food. Once the table was in sight, Jarek's stomach began to growl from hunger even more.

"Good evening, Mr. Videni," Annie said while sitting at her place at the table.

"Good evening, Miss Annie," Jarek responded back with a smile. "Ms. Smith," Jarek said with a nod gestured toward Rose, who was just setting the last dish on the table.

"Good evening, Mr. Videni," Rose responded flatly and without looking in Jarek's direction.

Jarek began to move toward his spot at the table when Annie interjected before he sat down.

"Oh, Mr. Videni, father won't be joining us this evening. He just came and took his plate to his office. Please, sit at his spot at the head of the table. Rose, please won't you join us and sit over there?" she asked, gesturing toward the spot Jarek himself had been sitting at each meal so far.

Jarek moved over and took his new spot at the head of the table. Rose stood just staring for a few moments before speaking.

"Thank you. Let me ensure everything is in order in the kitchen and the staff knows to leave once dinner cleanup is finished. You two go ahead and start eating without me."

Rose disappeared back into the kitchen, leaving Jarek and Annie sitting alone.

Jarek was waiting for Annie to take the first bite of her meal before he began to cut up the portion of pork loin awaiting him on his plate. As soon as her fork and knife sliced through a boiled potato, Jarek began to cut up the meat in front of him. He soon began to eat quickly so that his stomach might stop rumbling.

"You must be very hungry, Jarek," Annie said as she witnessed him devour the food on his plate.

Realizing his lack of table manners, Jarek paused his accelerated consumption of the food. "I am so sorry, Miss Annie. I didn't realize I was eating so fast," Jarek replied, a bit embarrassed.

"Quite all right," she replied with a chuckle.

"Actually, Annie, I am glad we are alone right now. I have an . . . unusual request."

Annie tilted her head a little, showing pure curiosity toward whatever Jarek was about to ask her.

"Certainly. Ask away."

"Well, I would like to attempt to make contact with your mother. I would like to conduct a séance. I think it would be the best way to help in this investigation."

"I—I don't know if that's a good idea, Jarek."

"I know there is only a small chance of making contact, but I was hoping you would join me. I would greatly appreciate you being there, and I believe that having your energy will make it easier for Sarah to make contact with us."

"I would certainly love to hear Mother again," Annie replied, suddenly sounding more optimistic at the opportunity.

"I make no promises, Annie, but I would like to see if she could help answer any questions in finding her killer."

"It might be worth a try. I know she would be able to help us."

"I agree," replied Jarek. "Now, it would be best if we could have one more person join us. It is best to have at least three people."

"Yes, I remember Mother saying that before when she would host such events here. But who should we ask?"

"I just had an idea," Jarek began to say, even though he already had the idea concocted. "What if we ask Ms. Smith? I don't know if she's ever done anything like that. However, she has such a close connection with your family that I believe her presence could help in reaching your mother's spirit."

"I think that is an excellent idea."

"You do?" asked Jarek.

"Yes, of course. I believe she has been part of a mediumship night, back when Mother would host them. Rose might be just the person we need."

"Need for what?" Rose asked sharply as she entered the room from the kitchen.

Both Jarek and Annie sat frozen as if someone were intruding during an intimate moment between two people.

"Umm," Annie hesitated.

"Well, out with it. I don't like people talking about me when I am not around," Rose said sternly, and she moved to her spot at the table and sat down.

"Well, Ms. Smith, Miss Annie and I were wondering if you would be willing to join us this evening for . . . well, for a social event." Jarek stated awkwardly, knowing that Rose was playing coy in order to not allow Annie to gain knowledge of her interest in Sarah's death.

"Excuse me? A social event?" Rose asked with her right eyebrow raised.

"Yes, Rose, it will be fun. Just like the old days," replied Annie.

"I'm sorry, but I am confused," Rose replied with a hint of befuddlement.

"We want to hold a meeting like Mother used to do. A chance to talk to the other side. We could invite many of Mother's friends," Annie blurted out excitedly.

Jarek got uneasy, as Annie was suddenly turning this opportunity into a much larger event than he had intended.

"Oh, I wondered if that was what you were alluding to," Rose replied. "I don't think we should invite company over now though. This close to the Christmas Eve party and all. Your father might not appreciate that."

"I agree with that, Ms. Smith," Jarek interjected. "This short of time until the party might cause additional . . . uh, additional stress on your father, Annie."

"I suppose you are both right. Then I don't need to hurry to get dolled up anyway."

"Very true. We can keep it to just us three. I am sure we will still be able to make contact," Jarek stated with hopefulness in his voice.

"So . . . if I were to participate, what is the intent of the contact? Who are we trying to reach?" Rose asked to help guide Annie to the same thought Jarek and she had.

"Well, Mother, of course," Annie replied with a hint of a condescending tone. "We could try to get some answers on finally confirming who killed her," Annie said while exhibiting some anger in her body language.

Jarek and Rose exchanged quick glances with each other. Jarek knew Rose was thinking the same thing as he was: Annie wanted to use this chance to finally confirm in her head that Martin was Sarah's killer.

"I think it will be a good chance to see if we can make contact, and perhaps we will get some answers to her death," Jarek said. "I believe it would be beneficial if all three of us would participate together in order to better our chances in communicating with Sarah. Would you be willing, Ms. Smith?"

"I am willing to do that. I have not participated in several months. My last one . . . well, was when Mrs. O'Connell was still alive. So if we make contact and I get emotional, please forgive me."

"No need to ever ask forgiveness for showing emotion," Jarek said.

Annie nearly cut off Jarek's sentence. "So it's settled then. We will hold a séance tonight. Oh, I am too excited to finish eating!"

Annie took her napkin and dabbed her face clean before crumpling it up and laying it on her plate. She began to stand up when she saw neither Jarek nor Rose stand.

"Well, what are you waiting for?" Annie asked.

"I need to finish my meal quickly. I am famished," replied Jarek. "Besides, we will need to prepare. We need to ensure your father is asleep for the evening, and I have a few items I need to gather myself."

"Oh," responded Annie. She looked like a child who had just had their favorite toy ripped from their hands.

"This will give you time to clean up from the day and maybe lay out your dress for the masquerade tomorrow evening," Rose said, attempting to turn the delay into a positive thing.

"That is an excellent idea. So, when should we do this?" Annie asked, appearing to calm down some.

"Well, I will go and check on your father in his study to see if he is getting ready to retire for the evening soon. He wasn't feeling . . . he wasn't feeling himself tonight, so it should be easy for me to get him upstairs and in bed," said Rose. "I need to ensure this dinner mess is cleaned up, too."

"How about we plan on meeting in the library at about eleven p.m.?" suggested Annie.

Jarek looked across the table at her. "I feel that is too close to your father's room, Annie."

"But that is where Mother would do her events!"

"I just believe it could hinder our chances of communicating with your mother if your father is too nearby," replied Jarek. "Perhaps we could do it in the parlor?"

Jarek suggested the parlor because it had given him the fewest feelings of the dark presence within the house.

"The parlor? But it is so cold and blank in there," replied Annie.

"I know, but it is the room . . ." Jarek paused when he realized what he was about to divulge and stopped himself. "It is the room I feel will give us the best chance."

"I think we should listen to Mr. Videni, Annie," said Rose. "He seems to be somewhat experienced. Certainly more experienced than you or I."

"Oh, all right. I will meet you both in the parlor at eleven p.m. Is there anything you need me to bring?"

"Just yourself and a clear and open mind," replied Jarek.

"OK, thank you, Jarek. I will see you in a few hours. If you need me sooner, I will be in my room."

"Excellent. I will see you then," said Rose.

Annie turned and left the dining room. Rose began to gather items on the table to bring them into the kitchen. Jarek stood up from the table and glanced out the door to ensure Annie had gone upstairs. He turned and placed his hand gently on Rose's shoulder and leaned in to talk quietly.

"All right, I will go to my room and gather a few things and prepare for tonight. I will venture down to the parlor at about ten thirty to get everything in order. I believe there is a small table in the corner and several chairs throughout the room we can use, right?"

"Yes, that will do. I will get this mess cleaned up and ensure the staff has gone home. Oh, and I will make sure Martin is asleep. If for some reason he isn't in his room, I will let you know."

"Excellent. I hope we get some answers tonight, Rose. We need to find some closure for Sarah," Jarek said as he gave her shoulder a gentle squeeze of assurance and then let go.

"We will, Jarek. I can feel it," Rose responded with a smile. "Oh, take these."

Rose moved over to the elegant buffet hutch. Behind the glass sat dishware of all fashions mainly made of crystal and silver. Rose reached in and grabbed two small silver trays and then leaned over and pulled open a drawer. She reached in pulled out a black velvet tablecloth.

"These were the burning tray, food tray, and tablecloth that Sarah often used when being a medium."

"Oh, fantastic!" replied Jarek. "On that note, do you happen to have any small treats to bring? Anything of Sarah's favorite?"

Jarek knew it was customary to offer a small portion of food at a séance. It was a gesture of good will to the spirits, and the smell usually helped to lure certain spirits if it was their favorite treat.

"Yes, I actually have some cheese biscuits. I shall warm a few in the oven before coming to the parlor later."

"Thank you, Rose. Truly, I mean it. Thank you."

Jarek grabbed the items from Rose and left the dining room as she went into the kitchen.

He began to cross the foyer toward the staircase. When he was at the foot of the stairs, he could suddenly hear the faint playing of the piano. He could hear the keys slowly playing the first few notes in the opening of "Carol of the Bells." It was only a few measures in when a slam of the keys by fist could be heard, which was then followed by the lid clearly slamming over the ivory keys. Jarek rushed from the stairs to the parlor. He crossed the threshold into the room.

No one was in sight. The room was empty. Jarek darted his eyes all around, looking at every corner. He looked under the furniture. Nothing, no sign of any person or thing in the room.

Suddenly, Jarek could smell a scent so foul. The strongest he had smelled since arriving. It was the same scent from the ballroom on his first night here, when Martin was giving him a tour. However, this was even more pungent and grotesque. Whatever was making that scent had just been in the room.

Jarek shook his head, mad at himself for not rushing faster to the room. He was also beginning to second-guess holding the séance in there. That room was their best chance of reaching Sarah tonight though. Or in reaching the young man he had already seen in the parlor. So Jarek took a breath, noticing the smell had dissipated. He took a sigh of relief and turned to go to his room.

Jarek hurried up the stairs. As he reached the platform of the second floor he could see Martin retiring to his bedroom for the evening.

"Goodnight, Mr. O'Connell," Jarek said loudly down the hallway. It was in vain, as the door could be heard latching shut.

"Odd," Jarek said lightly as he walked to his bedroom door and went in.

Jarek turned the knob, triggering the lamps to illuminate the room softly. He could immediately tell that something had been in his room. There was a certain energy throughout it making the tiny hairs on his arms and neck stand tall. It was a much better energy experience than the rancid smell down in the parlor.

Jarek's eyes glanced around the room. Nothing seemed to be out of the ordinary. He took a few steps further in. A draft of cold air came from the speaking tube near the door, sending a chill down Jarek's back. The chill made him shiver a bit. Then he looked at the fireplace, knowing he should light a fire since he would be up here for another ninety minutes or so.

While walking over to the small pile of logs next to the fireplace, Jarek noticed the flap on his satchel was flipped open. His eyes were then drawn to the table for some reason. It was blank as a new canvas. He turned back to grab a log to start building the fire.

The sound of rustling made Jarek turn back around. There, neatly laid out on the table, were his Tarot cards. It was the same six cards he had already revealed, just in a different order. Then, directly above them sat the oddest thing. A toad . . . Jarek thought it looked like the same toad he had hallucinated outside Dr. Monroe's office. He stood still in complete disbelief.

His eyes shifted back to the cards. The spread was presented in a straight line: The Hermit, The Hierophant, Temperance, The Magician, The Fool, and The Hanged Man.

Jarek took a step closer toward the table. As his feet moved, the fireplace suddenly ignited and began to crackle loudly.

"What the hell?" Jarek said out loud.

As the flames crackled, they began to cast shadows across the room. The Tarot cards looked different somehow, and the imaginary toad was suddenly gone, as if it never existed.

Jarek looked back at the cards, moving in closer to inspect them. The flames in the fire were casting shadows continuously in a pattern. He had never seen anything like it. How the flames hit Temperance and The Fool cards, they were almost unable to be seen. But The Hermit, The Hierophant, and The Magician completely illuminated by the flames. Jarek noticed The Magician was almost bright like a light, causing it to stand out the most. Then, cantered at the end of the row, almost as if not part of the spread, laid The Hanged Man.

Jarek stood observing the spread. His thoughts ran wild on what it could mean.

The mantel clock began to chime . . . one . . . two . . . three . . . Jarek assumed it must be 9:00 PM now. Eight . . . nine . . . ten chimes. Jarek turned his head and looked up. *How could it be ten p.m. already?* he wondered.

Time had been doing such weird things here. In fact, the continued bending of reality convinced Jarek that there was truly something sinister and powerful at work. Very powerful inhuman spirits were able to bend reality, often produce an unusually foul scent, and frequently leave totems . . . *That damn toad.* Additionally, the individual who conjured or helped the inhuman spirit cross into this world was attached to a familiar. A familiar is an entity—oftentimes disguised—who is actually a part of an inhuman spirit that was able to leave a part of themselves in this world. It finds a person strong in the dark arts and attaches itself to them in order for it to help amplify the person's power in hopes of fully bringing the inhuman spirit into this world. Jarek knew the mystery here was still deep, but starting to identify the dark entity was crucial to helping him in forcing the beast to release its grip on this home.

Jarek looked back down at the cards. He took a deep breath, collected his thoughts, and began to process what he just concluded in his brain. The fact that this house had an inhuman demon infestation and the meaning of the cards were helping him narrow down the person helping this foul creature in its endeavors. He was sure of it. Jarek took another deep breath, secured his satchel, and began to walk downstairs to the parlor. He was ready for the séance.

CHAPTER 10
SÉANCE

December 23, 1924, 10:49 p.m.

Rose was drawing the drapes in the parlor as Jarek was finalizing the table for the séance. Only a few of the oil lamps were lit in the room, with no electrical lamps turned on. The lack of electric light made the room dark and shadowy, perfect for the upcoming activity. Jarek retrieved a smudge stick from his satchel and held it above a flame from an oil lamp. The end of the smudge stick began to smoke. Jarek let it smolder for few minutes. He then proceeded to hand it to Rose. She walked the perimeter of the room, quietly praying under her breath, letting the smoke penetrate the air in the room. The process was leaving a calming scent and energy throughout the parlor.

Jarek finished arranging the three candles, the silver tray to rest the smudge stick on, and the other silver tray for the biscuits all on top of the black velvet tablecloth. Jarek then took one more piece of fabric from his satchel and wrapped it around the base of the candles to catch any wax that may drip during the event.

"Ms. Smith, can you retrieve the biscuits from the kitchen?" Jarek asked just as Annie was walking into the room.

"Certainly, Mr. Videni," Rose responded as she placed the smudge stick on the silver tray and walked out of the room.

"You were right, Jarek. This room might be better. It does feels right," Annie said.

"Thank you, Miss Annie. I have high hopes for tonight," Jarek said, looking at the young girl who appeared to be enthusiastic about the event. "I like that evening robe, by the way. It looks very comfortable."

Annie was wearing a blue silky night robe. It was very expensive-looking, soft, and flowing. Her dark brown hair was let down and clearly had just been brushed smooth.

"Thank you. I figured I better look like I was going to bed . . . just in case Father had seen me coming down here." Annie batted her eyes, displaying her long eyelashes in front of her emerald-green eyes.

"That is smart," Jarek replied, giving Annie a small debonair smile.

Rose returned carrying a small dish, followed by the heavenly scent of hot buttery cheese biscuits.

"Excellent, Rose! Just place a few on the other tray on the table," Jarek said.

Rose placed the biscuits down and leaned in to take in the smell herself.

The room was set up now, with the flicker of the flames from the oil lamps, the smell of smoldering sage, an offering of the spirit's favorite food, and the table set with candles ready to be lit. It was time to try and reach the other side.

Jarek moved and stood behind his chair, hands resting on the back. He took a moment to observe the room. The energy seemed to be all over. It was strong, just what he needed to conduct a mediumship. Yet behind it all lurked a darkness.

"Ladies, please come take your seats," Jarek said, gesturing toward the table.

Both women walked over to the table and sat down, Rose to his left and Annie to his right. They scooted their chairs in tight, right up to the table's edge. Jarek picked up a matchstick and struck it, causing it to ignite. He leaned forward and lit the three candles in the center of the table. He blew out the matchstick and laid it next to the smudge stick on the tray. Jarek pulled his chair out and sat down before scooting his own chair in close to the table.

"OK, please place your hands on the table so that we may join them," Jarek said, and the women followed the instructions and laid their hands into each other's, making a complete circle. "Feel and hear my breathing. Try to focus on that as you close your eyes and begin to breathe in unison with me."

The women's eyes closed, and Jarek began to feel them trying to join his breathing pattern.

Jarek closed his eyes. The room was nearly silent except for the faint sound of the three people breathing and the cold wind hitting the window outside, making a deep quiet howl as it bounced off the glass.

"Now, I am going to recite a chant to bring our energies out so that they may mix with the energy on the other side," Jarek instructed again. He then took a few shallow breaths before beginning the chant.

"In this tween time, this darkest hour, we call upon this sacred power. Three together stand alone, command the unseen to be shown. In innocence we search the skies, enchanted by our newfound eyes."

Jarek began to open his mouth again as both Rose and Annie attempted to join in.

> *In this tween time, this darkest hour,*
> *we call upon this sacred power.*
> *Three together stand alone,*
> *command the unseen to be shown.*
> *In innocence we search the skies,*
> *enchanted by our newfound eyes.*

The three individuals hoping to the find answers worked in unison while reciting the chant three times. It did seem to bring a feeling of connectedness in the room. The energies, though mixed, began to feel balanced. Jarek had tuned out the sound of the wind outside and the sound of their breathing. He could feel each of their warm hands in each of his hands. Not a sweaty warmth, but just as if they had each been holding on to a warm skillet right before touching Jarek's hands. This was all a sign of the energy in the room being high and ready. Jarek felt it was time to reach out.

"I am looking to speak with the lady of the house, Sarah O'Connell."

Silence.

"Sarah, my name is Jarek, and I would like to speak with you."

Silence.

"Are there any spirits here that can help us reach Sarah?" Jarek asked.

"I don't think . . ." Annie began to say before Jarek squeezed her hand.

"Annie, please remain silent," Jarek said quietly. "I am going to try communicating another way."

Jarek opened his eyes and glanced around the room. The two women sat still in their chairs, eyes closed tightly and holding hands. The rest of the room seemed the same as earlier, too. The sage still smoldered, the biscuits gave off a few streams of steam, and the candles flickered. He wanted to try a method he had read about that other mediums had used. The method used a combination of internal energy and attempted to pull in the surrounding energy to move him into a trancelike state. It was similar to how some spirits were able to make a full manifestation from the other side into this world.

Jarek closed his eyes and began to concentrate. He kept his breathing calm. He used all his might to pull the energy from within his core and project it outward. His body began to feel weightless, like he might pass out. Rose and Annie's hands still connected to his own, but it felt as if his hands were floating in midair. Jarek began to visualize Sarah and began calling to her spirit, asking her to make contact.

Silence. Then a slight knocking sound was made.

Jarek felt each of the women's hands squeeze his in startlement from the knock.

Another knock, another hand squeeze. Then another.

"Sarah, is that you?" Jarek asked.

Silence once again.

"Sarah, if that is you, please make your presence known."

Silence.

Right as Jarek was about to speak again, several keys on the piano seemed to be slammed out of anger. All three of them twitched from the sudden noise. Then the first few notes of a song began to play on the piano.

"Sarah, we hear you. We'd like to talk with you."

The keys banged as if someone slammed the hands down of whoever was playing the notes.

"Sarah, Sarah, are you still there?"

Silence.

A cool draft swept through the room near the floor, hitting everyone's ankles, causing Jarek to open his eyes. Both Rose and Annie still had their eyes closed. The room had not seemed to change at all, but Jarek knew something had happened. Something didn't feel right.

The chill from the cool draft quickly faded. The air became thick, still, and stagnant. It felt like how the atmosphere feels right before a storm. Jarek could feel the thickness and heaviness of the air on his face. His focus shifted down to the three candles lit in the table at the center. The flames stood perfectly still. No flicker, no nothing. Completely motionless. Jarek began to fully absorb his surroundings and realized everything within the room was at a standstill, as if time had stopped.

It worked. Jarek had moved into a dreamlike trance in the realm between worlds. He stood up to experience this ability further. As he stood up, he realized quickly how far into the realm he really was. Jarek looked around the room, then back at the table. He was looking at himself sitting in the chair still. He was not only in a trance, but he had pulled his consciousness out of his body and into the beyond.

Jarek leaned in toward the table, homing in on the candle flames. As he looked closer, he could still see a small moving flicker at the center. In this warm, thick, heavy air, time had not stopped completely but was rather just different. Jarek wondered if this difference in relation to time was how this plane always was. Could it be that this world between the living and the dead always moved at a slower pace, or was there simply just a difference between the plane. Or perhaps, just maybe, Jarek's trance worked, and he was able to summon a spirit strong enough to control the environment in which they wished to communicate.

"Hello, Jarek," came a voice from beyond what Jarek could see.

"Hello?" responded Jarek with a hint of nervousness in his voice. "Sarah, is that you?"

"Yes, Jarek. I am here."

A shadow emerged slightly from the foreground near the piano. It didn't have enough energy to become a full apparition, but Jarek could see and feel a presence in front of him.

"It is good to finally talk, Sarah," said Jarek as he glanced around the room to see if time was still moving lethargically.

"It's all right, Jarek. Rose and Annie aren't able to see or hear me. They don't . . . they don't have the abilities that you do, Jarek."

"How do you know about my abilities?" Jarek asked.

"On this plane between the worlds, it is easy to notice someone unique. Your very soul looks different. But that isn't important right now, I don't have much time."

"I need your help, Sarah. I need to figure out who killed you. And what is the darkness surrounding this house?" Jarek blurted out rapidly.

"Breathe, Jarek," the shadowy figure said as it moved closer to him. As it passed the piano, a few notes were played.

"I'm sorry, I just need your help so that I may help your family."

"And I greatly appreciate it, Jarek. They need your help. Help to bring them closure. Help Annie find her way in life."

"I will do my best, Sarah. But what happened that night, that night in the library?"

"I think you already know, Jarek. You know the answers to the questions you ask. You've seen how he is. He can be the best man you'd ever met; then the next moment, he can be hostile. He is battling a darkness within himself."

"You mean Martin is the one who did it?" Jarek asked with skepticism.

"Yes, Jarek. I love Martin, but he is not well. He is mad in his mind."

The shadowy figure seemed to fade a bit.

"Sarah?"

Silence.

"Sarah?" Jarek asked, reaching out from within and extending his arm toward her.

A semblance of a hand reached back toward Jarek's hand.

"I'm here, Jarek. I'm not going to be able to stay much longer."

"All right, Sarah, but please just tell me why. What did Martin do it?"

"I don't know, Jarek. I remember being in the library, and he came in so mad and angry. He was so confused. I tried to calm him down, but the next thing I remember is the sharp stabbing pain in my chest. His eyes . . . His eyes were dark. It was Martin, just not in the right mind."

The entity faded more, losing its humanlike figure.

"Help Annie. Help her to continue to learn, and lead her down the correct path in life . . ."

The voice trailed off.

"Sarah! Sarah!" Jarek shouted, arm still extended.

The dark shadowy arm extended back and grabbed his wrist. It sent a jolt through Jarek's body. It was a feeling so dark, filled with vast emptiness and despair.

Everything went dark. Dark . . . heavy . . . stagnant . . .

Jarek opened his eyes, unsure of how much time had passed. As he regained his focus, he could see both Rose and Annie still sitting there, holding hands in the circle. Candles were still lit, and he noticed they regained their natural flicker.

As Jarek stared at the ladies, they each opened their eyes almost concurrently.

"Well, that was a waste of time," blurted out Annie, clearly annoyed she didn't experience anything.

"Did neither . . ." Jarek paused midsentence. "Did neither of you experience anything?" he finally asked them both.

Jarek stayed silent as he began to process the encounter he had had. He immediately knew he must have been the only one to see or hear the being.

Annie released her grip from both Jarek's and Rose's hands.

"No, not a thing," Annie replied, disgruntled.

"Well, I heard the notes on the piano and could feel something happen," Rose responded quickly.

"Well, I'd hardly call that much of an encounter. Sorry, Jarek, but that was fairly pathetic. I expected more," Annie said angrily as she stood up from the table, pushing her chair back so aggressively it almost tipped over backward.

"I . . . I'm sorry, Miss Annie," Jarek responded with a dumbfounded tone, only making slight eye contact with her.

"Well, maybe next time. I shouldn't have gotten my hopes up so much. I just wanted to know for sure . . . but, like I said, I should not have gotten my hopes up. I just expected you to be better. To live up to everything . . ." Annie's voice trailed off.

Rose shot a curious look at Annie.

"Sorry, just frustrated," Annie said quickly.

Annie turned and walked right out of the parlor, leaving Jarek and Rose in dead silence.

Jarek sat in his chair, eyes wide open, but he was clearly deep in thought. He noticed that Rose, still sitting at the table, was staring at him. He cleared his throat.

"I'm sorry," he finally said after a few moments.

Rose didn't respond to him. She simply kept staring directly at him.

"What is it?" he asked.

"I'm sorry, Jarek. Even after everything you have seen since coming here, this is the first time that I have seen you scared," Rose said.

"That's because, for the first time, I feel scared."

"Why? Did you see something that Annie and I didn't?"

"Yes . . . I was frozen in time . . . talking to . . . talking to Sarah."

Rose took a deep breath and shifted slightly in her chair as she leaned toward Jarek, her elbows resting on the table. "Isn't talking with Sarah what you needed?"

"Yes. It is . . ." Jarek trailed off.

"Well, then what is it, Jarek?"

"The entity I talked to, it wasn't Sarah," Jarek said, looking straightforward through the flicker of the candle flames. He began scratching at his wrist.

CHAPTER II

SARAH

December 24, 1924, 12:06 a.m.

Rose sat in her chair, still looking at Jarek. She didn't say a word to him. She let him process the event he just went through. The room was still. A very light draft moved through the room, reminding everything in its path that it was still winter outside.

"Jarek, what do you mean that wasn't Sarah you talked to?" Rose finally asked, breaking the silence.

"I . . . I can't explain it."

"Well, at least try."

"She . . . It made contact with me. It seemed to be Sarah, though I never saw it fully manifest. It stayed in a shadowy form.

The voice was what I assume Sarah sounds like, and it knew everything."

"So how do you know it wasn't Sarah?" Rose asked hastily.

"I just . . ." Jarek stretched his wrist. "I just know it wasn't. It told me exactly what it thought I wanted to hear . . . And it was just too obvious of an answer."

"Too obvious?"

"Yes, it told me that Martin killed Sarah. It even mentioned Martin's 'mad mind.' But no, this didn't feel right. I know within my heart this wasn't Sarah. This was something much more malevolent."

"Well, what could it be Jarek?"

"Rose," Jarek said. "I think this was a demon."

Rose's eyes grew wide as she slowly stood up from the table.

"The same dark demon that has a firm grip on this house."

"How . . . How could a demon be here? I thought we were simply being haunted by some spirits . . . trying to hide the truth of Sarah's death." Rose said, clearly showing her anxiety escalating as she thought about the possibility of a demon within the house.

"I believe that Sarah's death was used to summon the demon itself, Rose. I don't know exactly how yet, or what demon or even why. But I know that it is all connected."

Rose stood there for a moment. Her eyes continuing to grow as she stared at Jarek.

"I . . . I just don't know if I can believe that, Jarek."

"Is it not possible?"

"If that is true, Jarek, that would mean that someone . . . someone in this household summoned a . . . a—oh, I can't even say it. And they used Sarah's death to do it. Ripping out her heart, but for what?"

Rose was wiping away the water that was beginning to pool in her eyelashes as her voice trembled. Nearly on the brink of hysteria, she slowly walked toward the archway to the foyer. Before leaving the room, she turned back toward Jarek with a face that looked to be filled with nothing but hopelessness.

"It's all right, Rose. We will . . ." Jarek paused.

The sparks of a small orb began to manifest in the archway just beyond where Rose was standing.

"Jarek?" Rose asked. "Jarek, what's wrong?"

Her voice began to fade in Jarek's ears, as he began to focus on the orb forming, growing larger and larger. It appeared to be the same one he had seen before.

Rose was looking at Jarek and clearly saying something, but Jarek was so tuned into the orb it seemed as if he suddenly had lost his hearing. A hum of energy grew louder as the orb moved past Rose, closer toward Jarek. He remained focused on it so intently, everything else seemed to disappear. He himself began to feel weightless once again, not hearing anything but the hum, not seeing anything but the orb. Then it got so close to his face, within arm's reach. Jarek extended his arm. The orb touched his outstretched arm.

Jarek felt an exhilarating rush throughout his entire body. A flash of light, then total darkness. He slowly regained his bearings. The air was still and cool. It seemed as if Jarek was standing in total darkness, yet he somehow could still see everything around him. The room, the table, the windows, and even Rose standing in the doorway. However, it all seemed to be transparent, as a mist slowly departing from the push of a slight breeze. Time was frozen again.

As he stood in the disappearing reality, he was face-to-face with Sarah. She was merely feet away, it seemed, nearly transparent herself, but Jarek knew it was her. Her presence was a calming energy for Jarek. He felt a combination of sadness and peace.

"Hello, Jarek. It is so good to finally speak with you."

Jarek, still stunned by what was happening, slowly began to open his mouth. "Hello, Sarah. I was hoping I would be able to speak to you."

"Yes, Jarek. I had tried making contact shortly after you arrived. Because of your presence, I finally began to gain enough energy in this world when you had just sat down for dinner, but I knew then was not the time."

"The orb in the dining room between Martin and Annie. That . . . that was you."

"Yes, it was. I wanted to give you just a glimpse so you knew you weren't alone."

"I felt it was someone good trying to reach me. I . . . I am glad I was right. But, what about in the library? Was that you too, Sarah?"

"Yes, Jarek. I needed you to see . . . To see that night and what happened. But the beast has such a hold on this house that I am limited in my capabilities. In fact, I won't be able to talk long. It will be able to stop me soon. Once it realizes we are talking Jarek, it will sever this tie."

"All right, Sarah, just tell me . . . tell me what I can do to help you, to help your family."

"The only way to help us is to release this house from the control of the demon, Jarek. It is the only way to uncover the truth."

"But where do I even begin, Sarah?"

"You already know, Jarek. You have the abilities within yourself to expel this being. You just need to figure out what demon it is to wield power over it. It was brought into this world through dark means. It was summoned using its seal and my death. It was then bound to this house using my heart and Samuel's soul as a tether. Only when you have expelled this darkness, only then can this house be let go and Samuel allowed to rest in peace."

"You have to too much faith in me, Sarah. I do not know if I am able to do what you ask of me."

"You were born with these abilities, Jarek. You being here is no coincidence. That much I do know. I can tell that you were born from light and darkness. But you have focused on the light, Jarek.

You are more powerful than you know. It pumps through your very veins."

"How do you know that? I don't believe I am more than what the eye sees," Jarek responded timidly.

"You're wrong, Jarek. I can see your soul. Your core is smoldering with potential. You just need to ignite that smolder and embrace the flame in order to extinguish this dark beast."

"I . . . I do not know if I can do that, Sarah. I am frightened I might not always use my abilities for good. I feel drawn to learning more about the darkness . . . it pulls at me. I worry if I give in any further, it will consume me." Jarek rubbed his face with his hands, trying to process what Sarah had said, and also realized he said out loud his own biggest fear.

"My boy, I have learned many things during my time on Earth and after. The most important thing we must do in life is to always seek out the good in each person, including the good within ourselves. Humans inherently have both good and evil within them, all people born to this Earth. But that is what is important, you see. For it is the people that realize this who are able to channel their energies into the good from within instead of letting themselves be consumed by hate and evil.

"Picture it like this, Jarek: Each person, from the moment of birth, has two small piles of embers within themselves, one good and one evil. With the right fuel and passion, these embers can become a small flame and grow to a raging fire. The goal in life is to ensure the ember of good receives the passion needed to become that raging fire and to never let the ember of evil become more than a small flame. Never let the anger or darkness of life fuel your embers, because the ember of evil can easily overcome the ember of good. And you, my boy, you were born with a unique and rare pile of embers. You were born to do something great, something to help this world become a better place."

Sarah took a pause. Jarek was silent from being in awe of this connection he had and from listening. He was consumed and enthralled by the words Sarah was speaking to him.

"Jarek, I know you are still figuring yourself out. You are worried you aren't strong enough. You are still trying to discover the full potential of your gifts. You need to figure out who you are as a man, trying to figure out your past in the hope of better predicting your future. You hope that once you find your father, the answers to the questions you seek will help you. That may be true, Jarek, but it isn't the time yet. The faith you have in your father, the faith that fuels your drive, is a false a hope.

"For you see, hope is not a person, it is a feeling. A feeling we all retain within ourselves. Hope is what is at the center of that ember of good. It simply needs a spark to ignite that feeling. We must find our sparks to ignite our own flame. Your spark is the fulfillment of using your gifts to help others, to better this world. It is not in the false belief of finding all your answers in the man that abandoned you as a child.

"If we put too much passion into chasing answers to questions like these, it can lead to being driven mad and igniting the wrong flame within. Don't ever let that happen, Jarek. Focus on helping others, focus on your potential, and you might just stumble upon the answers you seek anyway."

"But . . ." Jarek paused and took a breath. "You're right, Sarah. I don't know how, but you're right."

Jarek rubbed his face again, but this time to remove the tears rolling down both of his cheeks.

"It is time for me to go, Jarek. You know what must be done to help my family and Samuel. Help bring them peace. Rid them of this evil that they may go on to have the lives they deserve. I leave you with this, Jarek. You are never alone. As you discover the full potential of your gifts, do not be afraid to use them. Remember to keep that ember of good ignited within yourself, and always, always try to help others find their own spark, that they themselves can ignite their own ember of good."

"But Sarah, how do I uncover who this dark being is? I don't even know where to start."

"Go back to where I brought you before. The answer was within your grasp. Listen, don't hear. See, don't look. Go back to where this nightmare began. The answers are there . . . all of them."

Jarek stood in silence, wishing that he could ask her so many more questions.

"Goodbye, my boy, be strong." Sarah faded away as if it were all a dream.

Jarek remained motionless. He began to regain the visual of everything around him. The room once again had color, though it was still shadowy from the only light being provided from oil lamps and candles. His ears began to regain hearing, as if he were waking from a deep slumber.

"Jarek?"

"Ahem," Jarek cleared his throat.

"Jarek, are you all right?"

The sound of the stray cat screeching outside the window was almost unbearable to his ears.

"Good Lord!" Jarek exclaimed.

"That is just the feral cats at it again. But you, Jarek, are you all right? I thought I lost you there for a moment."

Jarek realized that his time with Sarah was only a small moment in time with Rose.

"Yes. Ah, yes, I am fine. I just . . . I got lost in thought," Jarek lied.

It once again was quite outside.

"The cats seemed to have made amends over their disagreement," Jarek said while flashing a small smile toward Rose.

"Yes . . . they do that sometimes," Rose responded, taking a breath, realizing Jarek wanted to change the subject of the conversation from being about him. "Well, Jarek, I believe it is time we get some rest. We have a big day ahead."

"Why, yes, it's Christmas Eve!" Jarek realized it was already past midnight.

"It is, and I have much to do in order to be ready for when the guests arrive later today."

"Certainly. However, I am not sleepy yet. May I bother you for a cup of tea? I would like to have a cup and maybe try reading for a bit to relax."

"Of course, please follow me to the kitchen. I will get a kettle ready to boil."

Rose turned and left the parlor, walking toward the kitchen. Jarek quickly snuffed out the candles and oil lamps. He retrieved the items from the table to bring to the kitchen.

When he arrived in the kitchen, Rose already had a kettle filled with water and was igniting a burner on the stove.

"Oh, please, just place those items on the table there," Rose said gesturing toward the table where Jarek had eaten breakfast.

"Certainly," Jarek responded, setting the items down. "Do you have any herbs instead of tea leaves by chance? I want to drink something to help relax my mind before going to bed."

"I do not have anything currently prepared. However, if you step back here, I have many herbs to choose from," Rose said, walking toward the back entryway that Jarek had seen the workers come in and out of.

Jarek rounded the corner to see a wonderful, though small, window conservatory. It appeared to be an oversized bay window made of solid glass, allowing for the plants to receive plenty of sunlight. There were many planters filled with lavender, chives, black basil, sage, ginger plants, chamomile, mugwort, rosemary, catnip, and many others Jarek did not recognize.

"Oh, this is wonderful, Rose."

"Thank you, Jarek. I have grown to become quite a herbologist," Rose said, clearly proud of her green thumb. "Now, what would you like in your tea?"

"Let's see. My grandmother made me a wonderful concoction of chamomile, black basil, sage, catnip, and ground mugwort."

"Wonderful. I have all of those ingredients. I will get the ground mugwort from the cabinet and let you gather the other herbs."

"Thank you so much."

While they gathered the items and waited for the water to boil, no words were exchanged. Jarek could tell that Rose wanted to ask more questions but that it'd be pointless. Jarek was not willing to talk about the events of the evening to anyone. The silence was finally broken from the scream of the tea kettle reaching the boiling point.

"Your water is ready," Rose said with a grin, knowing she was stating the obvious.

"Thank you, Rose," Jarek said, giving a small chuckle to acknowledge her statement.

"Well, I will let you have your tea. I really must retire for the evening, Jarek. I hope you get some rest. Trust me, everything will still be waiting for you when you awake."

Jarek nodded his head slightly with an upside down smile, knowing that Rose was all too right: There was much awaiting him in the day ahead.

"Sleep well, Rose. Get some rest."

"You as well, Jarek," Rose said as she started to leave the kitchen before turning back. "And Jarek . . . Thank you. Thank you for coming here. It means more to me to have you here than you know."

Rose left the kitchen. Jarek could hear the sound of her footsteps growing fainter as she crossed the foyer and proceeded up the staircase to her room. Jarek placed the herbs into a tea ball and placed it in the kettle to allow it to steep while he took the tea tray with him up to the library.

Jarek walked into the library to find that a few electric lamps had been left on. He placed the tray down on the side table and poured himself a cup. Once he picked up the cup, it felt warm in his hands. The smell of the concoction reminded him of home, or rather his grandmother Leona. It brought him comfort yet sadness, because he would not be with her this Christmas. This would be the first time not celebrating the holiday with her.

Jarek was reminiscing in his mind about the wonderful Christmases he has shared with his grandmother. He began to wander around the library while sipping on the tea. It was overwhelming to him to see so many books. He wondered in his mind if Martin or Annie had even come close to reading them all. It would take several lifetimes, he thought.

Jarek's eyes began to peruse the rest of the room once again in hopes of noticing something he hadn't previously. He was about to walk up the staircase to the loft when a shadow darted quickly across the room. The shadow moved fast and was gone as quickly as it had appeared, like a mouse trying to sneak past a sleeping cat.

Jarek's gaze stopped once again near the large Persian carpet. He wondered if he had missed something earlier. When looking at the carpet's placement, it seemed askew. Jarek noted how impeccable everything in the house was, and everything was arranged so perfect. However, this Persian carpet seemed to just be thrown down . . . as if to cover a large blemish on the floor. He quickly remembered there were oil markings under the far corner, where his vision had shown Sarah's heart. He had been so distracted from everything else he had nearly forgotten about that.

Jarek set his teacup down on a side table. He bent down and began to roll back the carpet, revealing the oil blemishes on the wood. He kept rolling it back. The spot was nearly six feet in diameter. He could slightly see portions of the symbol that Hamish had told Jarek about. Though whoever rubbed the markings away did do a thorough job.

An idea struck Jarek. He quickly lit the oil lamps in the room that were near the symbol. He then proceeded to turn out the electric lamps, creating a low shadowy light that danced along the floor. Jarek's eyes bolted toward the side table where he had last seen *The Lesser Keys of Solomon*. The book still sat there. He quickly moved over to the table and retrieved the book, then began to kneel on the floor, trying to determine some of the parts of the symbol. Jarek moved around the perimeter, hoping another angle might help.

Without much luck besides identifying a few points, and a portion that looked to be the remnants of something similar to an iron cross, his eyes noticed a few other outlines, but nothing as a total picture. Jarek thought of another idea and moved swiftly up the staircase. He leaned over the railing surrounding the loft and looked down at the blemish on the floor.

Finally, Jarek could see what he wished to be able to see. His eyes were able to make out the prominent parts of the symbol. Whoever tried erasing the evidence of the symbol did a poor job after all, and for that, Jarek was thankful.

He stared at the floor trying to burn the image into his brain, since he had nothing to sketch it with. He realized he had left his satchel in the parlor. He took mental note of the primary images that remained, then proceeded to visualize the circle around it in which a conjurer would have written the name of the beast it was summoning.

A creak in the floor broke Jarek's concentration. He looked around the room; he was still alone. He went back to looking at the floor from above, then flipped open the book still in his hand. As Jarek began to turn through the pages of the various sketches of demonic symbols that had been passed down for generations, another noise punctured his ears. It was the sound of a creak followed by an almost scratching sound, like when a dog digs its claws into the wood floor.

Jarek slowly closed the book and once again looked around the room. It was dark and shadowy, but he could still see that it appeared to be empty.

A gentle draft made its way through the room, rustling the curtains slightly and sending a shiver down Jarek's spine. There was a slight scent that made his nose crinkle. It was like when you catch the smell of a dead rotting animal on the edge of the street. He jutted his eyes toward where it seemed the draft and the smell came from—the corner of the room where the passageway linked the library back to Jarek's room. The passageway door was not in the same closed position it had been when Jarek had entered the library earlier.

Long, gruesome, inhuman hands were wrapped around the door's edge, keeping it open just a crack. The nails were yellow and cracked, like a stray dog's claws. Suddenly, Jarek's nose took in the rancid stench again coming from whatever was watching Jarek from this passageway. As his eyes focused a bit more on the dark slit, he could see the eyes. The light green eyes with slits like a reptile. Something not of this world was peering at Jarek through the opening in the door.

Jarek knew this being was the culprit behind the dark feelings he had felt since coming to the O'Connell home. It was this thing that seemed to be lurking behind the grandfather clock, behind every curtain and picture frame, and what had appeared to him in his dream the other night. The dream that ended with his wrist being bitten by the viper.

"I've got you. I've got you, you son of a bitch," Jarek muttered to himself.

Jarek made his way slowly down the staircase, never breaking his sight on the creature. He stopped at the bottom of the stairs for a moment, simply staring at it. He had to move his arm up to cover his nose. The smell was becoming unbearable to breathe in.

Another creak was made in the floor.

Jarek jumped as someone behind him placed a hand on his shoulder. He turned around quickly, ready to defend himself, only to see Martin looking at him with eyes that looked still half-asleep, and he was only wearing his boxer shorts.

"Jarek, you're still awake?" Martin asked quietly as he let out a yawn. "You really should be getting to bed."

"Yes, yes. I was just about head back that way," Jarek said as he peered back toward the passageway. The door was once again closed tight, and the creature had gone back into the shadows of the house.

"Well, come along. I must have been sleepwalking again. I woke up down in the parlor. Such a strange feeling, if I must say so. I never get used to it."

"Hmm," Jarek whispered to himself. "Yes . . . yes, let's get you back to your room and myself to bed. We have a long day ahead."

Jarek noticed Martin's body glistening from sweat, as if he had been exerting himself, or perhaps he had just had a nightmare.

The men turned out the oil lights in the library, and each went their separate ways in the hallway to get some rest.

"Goodnight, Jarek," Martin said before walking into his bedroom.

"Goodnight, Martin," Jarek responded as he heard the latch of Martin's door close.

Jarek entered his bedroom, turned the switch on to give the room some light, and shut the door. He leaned back against the closed door and glanced at the hidden door to the passageway. It appeared to be tightly sealed. He let out a quiet sigh of relief. Something still felt off to him though.

Jarek's eyes were drawn to the chair near the fireplace. There on the chair sat his satchel. He knew for a fact he had left it in the parlor. *Perhaps Martin retrieved it when he was sleepwalking downstairs*, Jarek thought to himself.

About to move toward the bed, Jarek took a deep breath. Then the gentle graze of a touch caressed Jarek's shoulder. He stood motionless. The caress was so gentle, as if when someone pets a sleeping dog. Jarek's heart began to race. He slowly shifted his gaze down to his shoulder . . . already knowing what he was about to see.

There, resting ever so lightly on his shoulder, stroking it, were the long inhuman fingers with yellow cracked nails. The hand was unnaturally protruding from the speaking tube near the doorframe. As Jarek stared, unsure of what to do, the fingers slowly retracted back into the speaking the tube, making a low, long scraping sound.

Once the scraping sound diminished, Jarek could hear a muffled breathing sound. He leaned slightly closer to the tube.

A whisper came from it. The voice you'd expect from a corpse if one were to speak. "No, Jarrrreeek, I've got you," it said.

A chill ran through Jarek's body from his head to his feet. He stood frozen for a few moments.

The room was so loud from absolute silence. Though still panicked from the events, Jarek knew he was the only one occupying the room now. Jarek began to breathe normally. He proceeded to place the book from the library under his pillow and then undressed for bed, all the while maintaining a watchful eye. He then turned the switch off and crawled into bed, still feeling that gentle stroking on his shoulder from the creature. Jarek closed his eyes and slowly, very slowly, drifted to sleep.

At least for a couple of hours.

CHAPTER 12

Preparations

December 24, 1924, 7:47 a.m.

Jarek's eyes opened wide.

"Mr. O'Connell . . . Mr. O'Connell. We need you downstairs please," said a voice.

It took Jarek a moment to realize the voice was coming from the speaking tube near the door.

"Mr. O'Connell, are you there?"

Jarek slowly crawled out from under his covers, only to expose his body to the brisk room. There was no fire lit in the fireplace, and the radiator heat was not nearly enough to warm the large room. Jarek quickly pulled the top blanket off the bed and wrapped it around his chilled body.

Jarek moved to the speaking tube and turned the knob.

"Ahem . . ." Jarek cleared his dry morning voice. "I'm sorry, but this is Mr. Videni. Mr. O'Connell sleeps in another room."

"Oh, my goodness. I am so sorry. I am new here. Please forgive me, I must have read this wrong down here . . ." The voice cut off.

"I am sorry, Mr. Videni. I hadn't shown him how to use the system properly yet," said a voice that Jarek recognized as Rose's.

"Quite all right. Nothing to apologize for."

"Oh, Mr. Videni. There is breakfast and coffee ready down here. And if you have time, please try on Mr. O'Connell's suit to ensure it fits well for tonight. I left a box outside your door with a mask for this evening as well."

"Thank you Ro . . . Thank you, Ms. Smith," Jarek replied.

Jarek moved to the fireplace and lit a few logs to help warm the room for a bit while he got ready. After the fire seemed to be stable, he turned toward the chairs and opened his satchel. He remembered it had somehow moved last night from the parlor to his room. He wanted to ensure all of the components were accounted for. It seemed as though nothing was missing; it was simply returned to him. However, upon a second look, he noticed the leather strap on his journal was not secured tightly.

Jarek retrieved the journal from the bottom of the satchel and opened it. He flipped through the pages slowly to see if anything stood out to him. Nothing seemed odd . . . and then Jarek stopped. On the last page, someone had written on the previously blank page: *You're finding the right answers. You know what to do.*

This note had just been written since last night. Jarek's first instinct was that it was Rose, but it was clear that the handwriting was different from the other notes he had been given during this case.

The only person whom Jarek thought may have moved his satchel was Martin. *But why would Martin write this note?* Jarek asked himself. Perhaps it was Peter. Or perhaps it was another person trying to help him, or another being.

"Mr. Videni, would you like us to keep the plate for you warm, or will you be skipping breakfast?" the new employee asked in the speaking tube.

Jarek walked over to the tube, turning the knob again.

"Keep it warm, please. I will be downstairs shortly. Thank you."

"Certainly, Mr. Videni. Again, sorry about waking you by accident."

Jarek didn't feel the need to reassure the new employee again that it was quite all right, so he looked back down at the journal in his hand. He reread the note one more time before closing the journal. He hurried to remake the bed sloppily, and then washed his face in the bathroom.

When Jarek stepped out of the bathroom, he remembered what Rose asked him to do. He obliged and tried on the suit that had been placed in his room the other day. It fit nearly perfectly. Martin was almost the exact same size as him. The only flaw was that the sleeves were a touch short, but Jarek figured that wouldn't matter at all.

Jarek removed the suit and placed it on the end of the bed. He put on his own clothes and was ready for the morning. He opened the door and found a small brown box with a black ribbon sitting on the floor. Jarek scooped up the box and placed it under his arm as he hurried down the hallway.

Once Jarek reached the platform of the stairs and looked down at the foyer, he felt as if he had overslept. The foyer was bustling with workers, Christmas garlands, and ribbons being placed all over. The smell of breads and meats cooking would satisfy anyone's sense of smell and get their mouthwatering.

Rose stood in the center of the foyer giving directions to people. She looked like an experienced conductor and was not remotely stressed over all the commotion.

"Oh, Mr. Videni. Good morning!" Rose said as she gave a wave and a slight smile in Jarek's direction but then proceeded to guide two men carrying a small pine tree into the ballroom.

Jarek zigzagged through the busy foyer and dining room, and entered the kitchen. He found the kitchen to be slightly less busy than the other rooms. Only two women were in there and were currently occupied with making rolls. The rolls baking made the room smell delightful. Jarek noticed that at the table sat Annie sipping from her coffee cup and reading the morning paper with her back toward Jarek.

"Good morning, Miss Annie," Jarek said cheerfully. "Merry Christmas Eve."

"Oh, good morning, Jarek! Merry Christmas Eve to you, too!" she replied just as cheerfully. "You slept well, I hope?"

"Yes, thank you. I got several hours of good rest. I'm ready for this evening's event! I have never been to a masquerade before," Jarek replied while moving to the table and sitting down across from her.

"Oh, you will love it. Here, let me pour you a cup of coffee."

"Thank you, Miss Annie."

"Of course. Now tonight, you likely will feel a bit out of place. Most of the people attending will be father's friends, businessmen from around here, and a few other people. It is so fun because it really does feel like a clip joint, to be honest." Annie paused for a moment before giving Jarek a sly smile. "Father and the local police . . . Well, they have an understanding about alcohol, if you get what I mean."

"Oh, I think I understand," Jarek responded with a smile.

"If it's like the years past, it really is a winging of a night. You will see firsthand the richest and brightest our city has to offer, and a few palookas thrown into the mix," Annie said with a laugh.

"Well, you certainly have intrigued me, Miss Annie. It is sure to be one of the high points of my journey here."

Annie gave Jarek a big smile and then proceeded to sip her coffee and read the newspaper. Jarek removed the lid on the covered plate in front of him to reveal his breakfast. He began to eat the fried eggs and sausages while looking around the kitchen at the other food already prepared for this evening. He was so impressed at the entire operation that was being run directly before his eyes.

Jarek took a pause in his amazement and looked across at Annie for a moment. She had her hair pulled back in a pewter clip and a face with just enough cosmetics on to bring out her natural beauty. Not overdone like some of the women he had seen in New York.

"I can feel your gaze, Jarek," Annie said in a flirtatious way with a grin on her face.

"I'm sorry, Annie," Jarek replied, blushing.

"Don't be. I will take it as a compliment."

The two returned to the hint of awkward silence. The only noise came from the women working away, not even talking to each other.

"Miss Annie, I am sorry last night that you weren't able to experience an encounter with your mother," Jarek finally said, breaking the awkwardness. However, he spoke in a hushed tone.

"It is all right, Jarek. It wasn't your fault. I just shouldn't have gotten my hopes up," Annie replied calmly, but with a bit of a snarky tone. "Well, I should be going. I have a few of my friends coming over soon to help me get ready for this evening."

"All right, Miss Annie. I will see you this evening, I am sure."

Annie stood up and began to walk out of the kitchen.

"Say, what time are the festivities tonight?" Jarek asked.

"I believe Father put five p.m. on the invites this year, but you might want to double-check with Rose."

Jarek gave a curious look, because he assumed Annie would know what time she should greet guests.

Annie smiled at him, insinuating that she knew he was confused.

"You see, Jarek, as a young woman, I can't expect to be right on time. I have to make an entrance after all," she said with a smile.

"I understand," Jarek responded, smiling back.

As soon Annie had left the room, he looked to see that the two women were not paying attention to him and working on the rolls for this evening. He then retrieved the book he had taken from the library from the inside pocket of his suit jacket and began to flip through a few of the pages.

The telephone began to ring, startling Jarek. The larger of the two women took a pan of rolls from the oven, wiped her hands on her apron, and then answered the telephone.

"O'Connell residence," she said. "One moment please," she said before setting down the receiver and exiting the kitchen.

Jarek pulled the newspaper from across the table toward him and set it over the book. Shortly after, the woman returned to the kitchen with Rose following close behind. Rose and Jarek gave small smiles of acknowledgment to each other before she picked up the receiver.

"This is Ms. Smith."

Jarek pretended to ignore the conversation by glancing over the front page of the newspaper.

"Hello, Mr. Eideen," Rose said as she turned her body a bit to rest her back against the doorframe. "Yes, everything is coming together wonderfully. The event this evening is going to be . . ."

Rose seemed to be interrupted midsentence. Jarek took a sip of coffee, pretending to not notice the conversation. It was rude to eavesdrop, after all.

"Yes, it will be an eventful time for sure," Rose continued. "Well, I really must be going. So much to do yet. I shall see you soon."

Jarek turned a page on the newspaper.

"Yes, yes. See you soon. Goodbye."

Rose hung the receiver up and turned to Jarek.

"Sorry about that. Just a guest making sure tonight's planned events are still on."

Jarek looked up with confusion.

"I believe that some still worried the party might not happen. They worry Martin . . ."

Rose paused and looked over her shoulder at the two women. She moved closer to Jarek and leaned over the table, resting one hand on it and one hand on the newspaper. Her hand was placed directly on the part of the newspaper that Jarek was using to conceal the book. However, Rose began to talk in a low voice. She hadn't noticed an object under the newspaper.

"They worry that Martin might not be well. I fear that his condition has led to rumors and rumblings about town. Nevertheless, I will continue to be a good representative of this household and ensure these people that he is still an honorable man."

"Yes, certainly, Ms. Smith. Poor Martin, but we shall all get through this," Jarek said, trying to reassure her.

"Of course, we will!" Rose said, talking at a normal volume once again. "Now, would you mind following me, Mr. Videni? I need your opinion on something."

"Yes, of course, Ms. Smith," Jarek responded.

Jarek stood up and secured the newspaper in such a way that he was able to grab the book and nearly wrap it inside the newspaper. The two moved from the kitchen, once again zigzagging through the many helpers organizing the many desserts on trays in the dining room, followed by the many workers moving throughout the foyer holding decorations and heading to their precise locations.

"I have never seen so many fresh flowers in the wintertime," Jarek said, noticing all the beautiful white and red flowers, and lush poinsettias.

"Mrs. O'Connell always insisted on special orders of green plants for the parties. She just loved having the fresh plants all about the home intertwined with the garland, the ribbons, and the ornaments," Rose said with a small smile.

She took a pause and looked around the foyer. Jarek couldn't tell if she was thinking back on happier times when Sarah was alive or if she was looking to ensure someone wasn't nearby. She then moved closer to Martin's office door. Before she turned the knob, she turned her head back toward Jarek and gave a nod, gesturing for him to follow her in.

The two of them moved quietly into the office.

"Close the door," Rose said as soon as Jarek entered.

Jarek did as Rose instructed. He then looked to see Martin's office . . . his haven. Jarek's heart felt heavy, as if he were a burglar with a conscience. But he could not help looking around at the beauty of this room he had not yet seen.

The architecture was similar to the parlor. It had a wall of bookcases immediately to the left and also off to the far right. The bookcases were elegant and ornamental, like those in the library. Directly in front of Jarek was a sitting area with a leather tufted sofa and two velvet chairs. There were two large windows directly across from the door that were adorned with beautiful emerald-green drapes. Off to the far right, in front of the bookcases, sat an extravagant desk with hand carvings of all sorts of creatures. The walls were adorned with a few sentimental items related to the print factory, but directly between the two windows was an oil portrait of the O'Connell family.

Jarek's gaze got lost in the painting for a moment. Martin, Sarah, and Annie all looked so calm and content. A sharp contrast to their current family situation. Jarek felt a wave of sadness come over his entire body.

"Beautiful family, aren't they?" Rose said.

"Yes, very beautiful," Jarek responded, gaze still lost in the portrait.

"I miss those days."

"I'm sure, Ms. Smith," Jarek said, changing his gaze from the portrait to Rose. "But that is why I am here—why *we* are here. We need to find the answers to bring closure to this home."

"You're right, Mr. Videni," Rose said with a tight-lipped smile, giving a nod with her head.

Jarek's wave of sadness suddenly turned to a fuel for the hope within him. The hope that he would be able to truly help find Sarah's killer and hold them accountable.

"We won't have long. Martin just had to go visit the print factory so he can give out the Christmas gifts to the employees."

"That is very kind of him."

"He does it every year. He usually delivers the gifts and then gives them the rest of the day off with pay."

"Martin is a generous man," Jarek said as he looked back at the painting depicting the family.

"Yes, he certainly is . . ." Rose's voice trailed off. "All right, I have to show you this," Rose said abruptly, changing the subject.

Rose crossed over toward the desk and began to rifle through one of the drawers.

"Here, look at this," Rose said as she drew a small leather-bound book from the drawer and laid it on the desk.

"What is that?" Jarek asked, already knowing it was likely Martin's journal.

"It's a journal. It belongs to Mr. O'Connell . . ." She trailed off, then looked up at Jarek. "Or rather, it belongs to Peter."

Jarek stared for a moment with his eyes beginning to widen.

"I found it this morning when I was in here cleaning up a bit. Martin never likes the staff to come in here because he keeps lots of sensitive documents for the factory here. So, he usually leaves the cleaning of this room up to me. When I was putting a stack of papers away in the drawer, I saw it. I was too intrigued and began to look through it."

"Ms. Smith, that is a massive invasion of one's privacy. Reading another person's journal is a large breach of trust and . . ."

"Oh, really, Mr. Videni. Get off your high horse and look at this," Rose said, interrupting him.

Jarek turned and looked back toward the door of the study.

"He won't be home for at least another hour," Rose said.

"Oh, all right. What did you find?" Jarek asked as he walked over to the domineering wooden desk.

"Here, look," Rose said as she held the journal so they both could see its pages. "He—well, Peter—has many entries in here. He talks about the accident between him and Martin at the mill as boys. He mentions all sorts of things as a child. But then these pages here . . ." Rose turned closer toward the end of the book. "He talks about how he wishes he could change the past. Mart—Peter says he wants to fix the accident. He goes on to talk about some dark methods of doing just that . . . talking to something powerful that can fix it. He just needs to know what to do, and he is willing to do it."

Rose paused for a moment, then turned one more page, revealing a symbol that matched the same one Jarek had already deciphered to have once been on the floor of the library.

"I don't like the look of this," Rose said. "It appears that Peter was dabbling in the dark arts."

"It certainly appears to be that way," Jarek said, never breaking his gaze from the journal. "May I?" He took the journal and flipped through the pages preceding the symbol, then flipped through the pages after it.

"I never thought that Martin could . . . that he could ever do something like this."

"Stay calm, Ms. Smith. There may be an explanation for this." Jarek took a long pause. "Or we may have been wrong about Sarah's true killer."

The two of them stood quietly in the study for a moment. Then there was a soft knock at the door. Just before it opened, Rose secured the journal and slid it back into the drawer quickly.

"Excuse me, Ms. Smith. We need your direction in the ballroom," said a young man as he stuck his head into the study through the slightly open door.

"Certainly, Ronald. I will be right out."

The young man retracted back to the foyer, closing the door the behind him.

"We should be going. I have much to do before this evening," Rose said as she began to walk toward the door.

"Is there anything that you will need assistance with today?"

"No, Mr. Videni, you have your hands plenty full. Go about town or relax in the library. I am afraid the entire main floor is going to be quite busy all day, and I will be just as busy." Rose opened the door, once again allowing the bustle from outside the confinement of the study to penetrate the room.

"Oh, don't worry about me, Ms. Smith. I rather like to be a brooder at times when I am conducting research. I find it helps me to be a fairly swell snooper."

Rose looked back at Jarek, nodding her head to acknowledge his work on the case ahead. Jarek returned a small smile and wink to her before she went back to the many duties bestowed upon her for this important day.

Jarek adjusted the newspaper that concealed the book under his arm. As he left the study, he turned and looked at the oil portrait of the loving family one last time. He then pulled the door of the study until he heard the latch.

Ж

Jarek looked in the mirror as he carefully shaved his face in preparation for the event this evening. After spending time in his room looking through the book, he decided he better begin to get ready for the party. The sun was still shining out but was beginning to set for the day. The cold wind blew outside the windows in the bedroom. Jarek could hear the soft howl from where he stood in the bathroom. There was a slight fog around the edges of the mirror from the warm water that countered the cooler room temperature. Jarek had never experienced being in a home that had its own scuttle-a-day tank. He had only known to heat water in the kitchen first and then bring it to the bath. He was impressed. Feeling the warm water coming directly from the water fixtures made him feel like royalty.

Jarek finished shaving his face and began to draw himself a warm bath. While the bathtub was filling with water, he went and retrieved the book he had taken from the library and returned to the bathroom. He set the book on the small table that was arranged next to the oversized iron claw foot tub.

The warm water hitting Jarek's feet as he entered the bathtub immediately began to warm his entire body. Though the O'Connell house had radiator heat and fireplaces throughout, Jarek still felt a chill in the bathroom. He blamed the chill on the fact that the home was in a location much colder than where he came from. Minnesota cold was drastically different than the cold that hit New York City. He also considered the fact that his body was continually on edge in this home, giving him chills often.

Jarek sank down into the water as far as he could, then placed a towel behind his neck on the edge of the tub. He reached over and grabbed the book off the small table. He began to turn the pages depicting the seals that belonged to each major dark being that filled the ranks of hell's formations. Unsure of what dark being was occupying the O'Connell home, he began to flip from page to page. Jarek initially had doubts he would find out the identity of the demon, but when he saw the image in Peter's journal, he knew he had seen that seal before in remnants on the floor of the library.

He continued turning pages slowly, but nothing matched.

The sound of deep shallow breaths began to hit Jarek's ears. They sounded far off yet gave his body a chill because he could feel them coming from something close to him. Jarek looked up slowly from the book, trying to see through the small crack of the bathroom door that was slightly ajar into the bedroom. There was no movement out in his bedroom, but he knew something was there.

Taking a deep breath himself, Jarek assumed he was being watched at every moment, and right now was no different. It could be the demon itself or something else it had lured into the home or poor Samuel's spirit wandering aimlessly about. Until Jarek had what he needed to wield power over this beast, there was nothing he could do about it. The feeling and sound of whatever was out there dissipated.

Jarek's fingers turned another page in the book, and his eyes shifted back down toward the pages. There it was, right before his eyes—the seal of the demon. It matched what he could see on the floor of the library and what was drawn in Peter's journal. The symbol that disclosed everything Jarek needed to know about who it was, what it did, and its known strengths and weaknesses.

Jarek quickly closed the book, once again hiding the pages that bore the information he needed. He set the book back on the small table and then sunk a bit further into the warm water until it covered his chest and was touching his neck. His eyes grew heavy as the warm water relaxed his body, and knowing he just gained a major piece of the puzzle relaxed his mind.

As Jarek's eyes closed, his mind began to wander. He began to think about being home back in New York. He wished his grandmother was able to travel with him. He knew she would have already been able to solve this case. She would have found Sarah's killer and known why Sarah was murdered.

Jarek's mind drifted into sleep while trying to process this mystery and visualize what he had seen in the vision from Sarah. Jarek's body went limp in the water. Feeling weightless, the water seemed to be consuming his body the further he drifted away. His mind became blank.

"Jarek, listen to me."

Jarek's eyes shot open.

"Jarek, listen to me."

Jarek was confused. His eyes were open, but he was in a completely empty space. There wasn't anyone verbally talking. Jarek took a deep breath and reevaluated his senses. He felt the words from someone instead of hearing them. Jarek closed his eyes and took a quick moment to process what was happening. When he opened his eyes again, it was dark, yet he could somehow see. It was neither cold nor hot. He was there but couldn't even see his own body when he looked down. Suddenly, he began to see everything, all the clues laid before him. Someone was making him see. Martin's words, Annie's words, Rose's words, Sarah's words, the vision in the library, the Tarot cards, and every other interaction he had witnessed since arriving in Saint Paul—every piece of the puzzle had been placed before him. He listened, he felt, and he understood.

When Jarek opened his eyes, his body was shivering from the cold water that now filled the bathtub. He knew some time had passed. He noticed while looking out the crack in the door into his bedroom that it was fairly dark.

Jarek stood up and left the cold water behind as he walked over to the towel hanging on the back of the door. He dried off a bit and then wrapped the towel around him and walked over to the sink. He turned on the hot waterspout and let it run for a few moments. He wanted to splash a bit of warm water on his face to warm up his nose and cheeks. He moved his head down toward the hot water and splashed it on his face several times before looking up at the mirror.

The steam from the warm water had fogged the edges of the mirror. Jarek could see portions of letters there written by a small finger, probably that of a child. He took a deep breath and huffed on the mirror, causing it to fog entirely to reveal the message that someone had written while he was asleep in the bathtub:

It'll happen again tonight
You're next

Jarek reached for the small hand towel and used it to wipe the mirror clean of the steam, erasing the message. He threw the hand towel to the floor in anxiousness, turned, and grabbed the book on the small table. He walked out into his bedroom and looked around. Nothing seemed to be out of the ordinary. He shoved the book into his satchel, then walked over and placed a few logs on the fire and reignited it to help warm the room again.

While getting dressed in the suit, Jarek realized he had not been to a party in quite some time, let alone a party of this extravagance. Too bad it was overshadowed by this darkness and his duty to see to its end.

The suit was a nearly perfect fit, except for the short sleeves, of course. Jarek laced up his boots and gave them a quick shine with the hand towel he had thrown to the floor in the bathroom. He then grabbed the bow tie and small box off the table near the chairs and fireplace. He went back into the bathroom to use the mirror and tie the bow tie perfectly.

Jarek oiled his hair and slicked it back. He opened the small box and pulled out the black mask inside that Rose had given him earlier. He placed it over his face, pulled the strings back, and tied them tightly so it wouldn't slip down.

He looked back into the mirror to see how he looked, but there in the reflection standing behind him was the faint reflection of the boy with the sewn mouth. The boy was looking at Jarek helplessly, motionless. It dawned on Jarek that the message written on the mirror had no malevolent intent; rather, Samuel was warning him of the demon's plans. The boy was bound from communicating with Jarek . . . at least verbally. He gave a small grin and nod to the boy, acknowledging his cleverness.

He then looked down by the sink. The six Tarot cards were sitting there in a pile. Jarek looked at each card. They were arranged exactly in the right order. Samuel had the answers all along. The boy had just outsmarted the demon and validated Jarek's detective work.

Now it was time for Jarek to confront the demon. It was finally time to pull the mask off the person responsible for killing Sarah and bringing this darkness into the world. It was time for the masquerade to be over.

CHAPTER 13

MASQUERADE

December 24, 1924, 5:39 p.m.

As soon as Jarek opened the door into the hall, he could hear that the noise of the evening's activities had started: people talking and a string ensemble playing music. The smell of the food wafted throughout the home. Jarek walked down the dark hall toward the light beaming up the stairs from below. Happy sounds grew louder with each step, and he enjoyed taking them in. He had not heard them in a very long time, and he was sure the same was true for the family.

Jarek reached the platform on the stairs overlooking the grand foyer. The garland and ornaments ordained the railing and every door. There were workers taking coats from guests that arrived, workers walking around with platters of many foods and sweets, and a few workers had platters with drinks—clearly prohibited drinks, but they overlooked for an evening such as this. Then Jarek's eyes caught what he was looking for. There, near the grandfather clock, stood the O'Connell family. Martin wore a black dinner tuxedo jacket, a gold bow tie, and his hair was oiled and combed perfectly. His prominent jawline was even more pronounced with his clean-shaven face and a black but elegant mask, which was identical to the one Jarek was wearing. Martin looked up at Jarek and gave him a smile, as if he were proud of the fact that Jarek had an expression of awe at the sight of the party.

Annie stood next to Martin, greeting newly arrived guests. She looked majestic in her dark black trumpet dress with gold lace embellishments. Her dark hair was in an updo with black feather accents. She wore an elaborate black-and-gold mask with lace and feathers. Annie's long thin arms were nearly covered with long black gloves. The two of them looked like royalty to Jarek—a family of pure elegance.

Behind Martin and Annie stood Rose. Clearly proud of the unfolding evening thus far. She was smiling, pretending to half-listen to the conversation Annie was having with the guests. However, Rose kept taking glances around the room, ensuring the workers were doing their jobs and that the guests were happy.

As Jarek took his first step down the final flight of stairs, the string ensemble began to play a new song. He walked over to the elegant family just as the guests were finishing saying their hellos to them.

"Jarek, we were beginning to wonder if you were going to join us this evening," Martin said jokingly. "I was about to come check on you myself."

"Oh, stop it, Father," Annie said while giving a quick roll of her eyes.

Jarek smiled and gave a slight bow to greet them for the evening. "Mr. O'Connell, Miss Annie, you both look amazing this evening," Jarek said.

"Thank you, Jarek. You look all right yourself," Martin said, still thinking he was quite funny, Jarek assumed.

"Father, stop. He looks very dashing. He certainly looks better than you," Annie said, retaliating for embarrassing her in front of Jarek with his unfunny jokes.

"I was being sarcastic, Annie. Lighten up; don't be so serious. Tonight is a celebration," Martin said as he placed his hand on Jarek's shoulder and gave it a tight squeeze. "In all honesty, Jarek, you do look better than me. You clean up very handsomely."

"Thank you, Martin," Jarek responded as he returned the shoulder squeeze.

"Wonderful! OK, I think that was the majority of our guests, Annie. Shall we go into the ballroom?" Martin asked her while holding his arm out for her to take.

"Lead the way, Father," she said as she took his arm, and they walked to the ballroom together.

Jarek stood still while watching them venture toward the opened doors of the ballroom.

"And how do you know the O'Connells?" asked an unfamiliar female voice.

Jarek turned to see it was the couple that had just been talking to Martin and Annie a moment ago. They were a man and woman, likely in their midfifties, and dressed fairly well-to-do.

"I, ah . . . I am here helping them with some personal matters."

"Well, don't get too specific," the man responded, laughing at Jarek's vagueness.

"Sorry, it is a just a sensitive topic."

"Oh! You're helping with the investigation into Sarah's death!" the woman said excitedly.

"That explains the lack of an answer," the man said.

"Yes, that would be correct," Jarek said.

"I hope you help find the killer. Honestly though, I wasn't too surprised when it occurred," the woman said frankly.

"What do you mean, you weren't surprised?" asked Jarek.

"If you don't mind me saying, I loved my dear friend, and I love this family. However, sometimes . . . Well, let's just say they appear to be a few eggs short of an omelet," the woman said and then proceeded to chuckle, soon joined by the man she was with.

"Yes, they get a little aloof and involved in that spiritualism stuff. It was bound to attract some very seedy people," the man said.

"Have you ever noticed anyone seedy in particular?" Jarek asked, intrigued.

"Oh, my, no. We have never come to any of their nights. So I am afraid we won't be much help in your investigation," the man said quickly.

"Well, it was wonderful to meet you . . . ?" the woman said while extending her hand out.

Jarek returned the outstretched hand. "Videni, Jarek Videni. Wonderful to meet you both as well."

"It's been a pleasure, Mr. Videni. We are Mr. and Mrs. Nelson." the man said while giving a look toward the woman. "Well, Lydia, we really should go into the ballroom."

The woman nodded her head toward Jarek, then grabbed her companion's arm and followed him into the ballroom.

"Humph," Jarek said quietly to himself, still focused on the facial expression the man gave the woman.

"Never mind them. They are an obligatory invite to these parties," Rose said as she moved closer to Jarek. "Mr. Nelson is this city's mayor, and his wife Lydia is very active in all the social organizations."

"Ah, it seems their relationship with the O'Connells was cordial at best."

"At best." Rose laughed at herself a bit.

"Ms. Smith, you throw a hell of a party. This is certainly the best I have ever attended, and I haven't even been into the ballroom yet."

"Well, thank you, Mr. Videni. I appreciate that."

The two stood in the foyer for a bit, admiring everything around them. It was full of energy and life, yet it felt full of contentment. Something Jarek was sure Rose had not felt in a very long time.

"Samuel would have loved to be at a party just like this again," said Rose. "God, I miss him so much, Mr. Videni."

"Ms. Smith, I must tell you something about Samuel."

"Mr. Videni, I know children oftentimes think they are good at hiding secrets from their parents, but I know that Samuel was . . . born different. He had special gifts and abilities that I will never fully understand. And I know that he may have had other interests as well . . ." Rose trailed off for a moment. "And I will never understand that. But the best part about being a mother is that from the moment our children come into this world, our love expands exponentially. I know I don't have to understand everything about Samuel in order for me to still ensure he received that love from me. That, Mr. Videni, is the most beautiful and best part of being a mother."

"You are great mother, Ms. Smith. Both of your sons are lucky to have had you."

Rose smiled.

"I do have two favors to ask of you."

"Certainly, Mr. Videni."

"First, I do expect us to be able to find all the answers we need to bring true peace to this house once again. By doing that, you may hear and see many things that you cannot explain. I need you to not be frightened, to not listen to the vile entities that might make themselves known, and lastly . . . when you see Samuel—"

"See Samuel?" Rose asked, interrupting Jarek.

"Yes, Ms. Smith. For you see, his spirit has been bound to this house for some time and has been silenced by the demon drawing power from it. Samuel will need all of our strength to help break that binding that has been placed on him. He needs his voice returned in order to move on from this world."

"My boy," Rose said suddenly, trembling as her eyes became watery.

"I think you have known he has been here. He has been by your side. You told me you had felt his presence."

Rose was wiping tears away with a small handkerchief because she likely didn't want to ruin the cosmetics around her eyes.

"I have felt him. I've felt his presence. But I just figured it was from my grief, wishing he were still with me. Not that he was actually here."

"Samuel has been here this whole time. I will need your help, your hope, your strength, and your love to help him move on from this world. His time is long overdue and he knows it. Samuel will need you to acknowledge it, too, so that he has no guilt in leaving. Can you do that for him, Ms. Smith?" Jarek placed his hand on Rose's shoulder and looked directly in her eyes.

"Yes, Mr. Videni, I will do my best, and I will help in any way that I can." Rose gave Jarek a small smile through her tears.

"Now, secondly, there is a boy in this town—Hamish."

Rose's eyes widened a bit. "Yes, I know of him. He was friends with Samuel. He's the one I mentioned at the cemetery that would have Samuel coming home crying," she replied.

"Yes. Well, he currently doesn't have much love given to him at his home. Your son Samuel found room in his heart to love him. It is too much to explain, but trust me. I need you to share your love with Hamish. Can you do that for Samuel? Hamish needs someone in his life who shows they care about him." Jarek gave Rose's shoulder a squeeze.

"Yes . . . I think I can do that, Mr. Videni. For Samuel."

"Thank you, Ms. Smith," Jarek said as he leaned in and gave Rose a hug, which she graciously returned. "Now we must not be rude to the guests. It's time for a ball!" Jarek said, grabbing Rose's arms and leading her to the ballroom.

The evening continued to be a pleasant one for everyone attending, as far as Jarek could tell. The many guests—Jarek estimated nearly one hundred—were all laughing, eating, drinking, and enjoying themselves. Every person whom Jarek looked at was dressed elegantly. It was an eclectic group of people. Some guests seemed to keep to themselves or in small groups, and there were several people who seemed to know all of the guests. Jarek noted there were plenty of sniffers, and certainly everyone there were scofflaws. He didn't mind, or judge people for wanting to have a good time. Rather, it was just unusual for him to see since he was not from an affluent world. Most of his interactions with people seeking his help in the past came from those unable to afford the luxury of being overlooked by the authorities.

    Jarek spent the past few hours interacting with some of the guests, observing the key players in this entire situation, and primarily keeping his senses in tune in case something arose. Something about this evening seemed too pleasant, and it led Jarek to keeping his guard up even higher.

    Through the few short interactions Jarek had with attendees, he was able to deduce they were business officials and elected officials from the area, just as Annie and Rose had said. No other family members, and certainly no close friends. The O'Connell family was small. Both Martin and Sarah were only children in their families, and all of their parents had passed on. Jarek had determined that this was exactly why something dark would target this family. Some of these beings believed that the smaller the family, the easier it was to consume them without others noticing. However, Jarek knew that was simply a weakness of dark beings. Rather, it depended on each person's individual strengths and the people they surrounded themselves with that made them the most vulnerable.

"You look lost in thought, Mr. Videni," Annie said as she broke Jarek's concentration on the room filled with people.

"Oh, just admiring the room and all the people, Miss Annie. This certainly is the bee's knees," Jarek said with a smile.

"Isn't it though?" Annie said as she looked around the room with a proud disposition.

"I have never been to something so extravagant, nor have I been around so many beautiful people in one place."

"Why, thank you again, Mr. Videni," Annie said while giving Jarek a quick flutter of the eyes. "I am certain Father will be speaking soon. He usually gives the guests a thank you for coming right before telling them to get the hell out by midnight—jokingly of course." Annie said, laughing.

"I am certain the guests would stay until morning if they were allowed."

"Oh, trust me, they have in the past. I have always loved these parties but also disliked how rambunctious the nights can become."

"I can only imagine," Jarek said with another smile.

Just then the music began to grow quieter, and Martin could be seen walking up toward the Christmas tree in front of the oversized windows. He had a glass of champagne in hand. The guests began to hush, already knowing that Martin was going to address them all.

The room was silent. Martin, standing in front of the Christmas tree, faced the crowd and raised his glass. "Thank you all for joining us here tonight! This is the most life and energy we have had here in far too long. This home has been too quiet for too many months."

He took a pause, clearly holding back emotions.

"Tonight is about celebrating, about another year coming to a close, and about being together with friends. This year has been a tough one for my family. However, one thing I know: I could not have survived this dark time without my daughter. Annie come up here," he said as he extended his arm toward her.

Annie, blushing slightly and patting Jarek's arm, left his side and moved through the applauding crowd toward her father. She got to him and touched his outstretched arm as he pulled her in tight. Martin raised his glass of champagne back in the air and looked out toward Jarek.

"So let us raise our glasses. This is to new friends, to bringing 1924 to an end, and to finding comfort in those who stay by our sides."

Everyone clanked glasses in cheers.

"All right, everyone, get back to the party! Remember to be out of here before midnight, and have yourselves a wonderful Christmas!"

The room returned to applause for a bit before the orchestra resumed playing music, and people began their conversations again. Jarek's cheeks began to blush. His arms and legs began to tingle. All of Jarek's senses began to feel different. He began to move his head around the room. Something had entered. Something was watching. Jarek moved his gaze back toward the front of the room to the massive Christmas tree in front of the large windows. Martin and Annie were embraced in a half-hug, looking genuinely happy. Rose stood off to the side, looking at them hugging with a smile on her face. But behind them all, Jarek could see a dark aura. A dark shadow beginning to slowly consume the entire front of the room. Everyone seemed to be totally unaware, except Jarek. Then all three people in front of the tree turned their heads and looked at him.

Jarek realized his facial expression must have disclosed there was something wrong, because they all looked concerned, exchanging clearly confused gazes with him.

The shadow behind them began to twist and turn. It was crawling up the walls and windows, slithering around the tree. Then it began moving downward, as if to disappear directly into the floor.

Jarek quickly covered his nose with his forearm as that unmistakable stench began to seep into his nostrils.

Rose walked through the crowd over to Jarek. "Mr. Videni, are you all right?"

"Yes, yes, I am," he said, bringing his arm down.

The smell started to dissipate.

"You looked at if you've seen a ghost."

"Certainly not a ghost," Jarek responded. "But I think it is getting close to the time, Ms. Smith. I can feel it."

Rose's face changed to a look of fear and sadness combined. She likely was not mentally prepared for what needed to be done. Jarek took her hand and gently squeezed it to give her reassurance.

"It will be all right, Ms. Smith. I am going to need you tonight. You knew this time would come."

"Time for what?" Annie asked as she walked over, overhearing just the end of Jarek's sentence.

"Ahem." Jarek cleared his throat. "Well, time for some more dancing, of course."

"Yes, Annie, why don't you go ask your father for a dance?" Rose suggested.

"Yes. Martin, won't you come here?" Jarek yelled over to Martin, who was still standing near the tree.

Martin gestured an acknowledgment with his hand, then proceeded to walk over to them. "What can I do for you, Jarek?" Martin asked with a smile.

"We were just thinking it would be an excellent thing for Miss Annie and you to share a dance."

"Just like in the past when Sarah and you would share a dance during this very party," Rose said.

"I think that is an excellent idea. Annie, won't you join me?" Martin asked as he made a slight bow while extending his hand for her.

Annie didn't say a word. She reached out and took her father's hand. Martin led her to the area near the orchestra. Martin went up to the musicians and talked to them briefly. Jarek assumed it must have been a special request for a certain song. Martin moved back down to Annie, held her hand, and took his position, ready for the music to begin.

As soon as the orchestra began playing, Jarek recognized the song as a newer popular one: "What'll I Do?" The guests all gave the two of them space to dance. It was a special moment for all to witness and likely brought back many memories of Sarah for everyone in the room.

The next few minutes, everyone simply watched the pair dance. The guests continued to sip from their glasses, some muttered a few words to each other, but most of them just enjoyed watching. When the song concluded, Martin and Annie gave each other a big hug, clearly emotional.

The room began to rumble with applause. Martin took a few bows, while Annie curtsied.

"Thank you, thank you!" Martin said as he waved to his guests. "Jarek, please join me!" Martin shouted over the applause.

Jarek looked caught off guard, but obliged and began to move toward the dance floor.

"This man here, Mr. Videni. Give this man recognition."

The guests all clapped, unsure of why. Some talked among themselves, drinking more booze before the night was over. A few guests took sniffs from tiny containers to continue their high.

"This young man has given up his holiday to be here with us. He is here to help with Sarah's case. And though he hasn't been able to solve it yet, just having him here has brought my family comfort and rekindled the hope we have in bringing justice to Sarah's death. From the bottom of my heart, Jarek, I thank you, and I know that Sarah thanks you."

The guests all began to clap again.

Jarek noticed Rose wiping away a few tears with her handkerchief before removing herself from the room entirely, exiting through the door to the kitchen.

"All right, everyone, all right! You do not have to go home, but you can't stay here!" Martin told the guests as they all laughed and applauded in thanks for a wonderful evening.

The guests were starting to leave as the musicians continued playing Christmas carols softly in the background. Many of the guests where thanking Martin and Annie for their hospitality, while some guests simply ducked out quickly. A few people gave Jarek nods as they walked past him. Jarek didn't know if it was simply a goodbye or a nod to acknowledge that he was here to help solve the case for the family.

As the final guests exited the ballroom, Martin closed the double doors leading to the foyer. "All right, it is time for one last special dance . . . Annie? Jarek? Would you do me the honors of giving us a dance?" Martin asked them both with each of his hands extended to them.

"Certainly, Father," Annie said with a big smile. Her eyes behind the mask seemed to sparkle at the thought of being the center of attention again and getting to dance with a handsome gentleman.

The room's atmosphere began to grow heavy to Jarek again. Something did not seem right.

Jarek took Martin's hand, Annie took the other, and Martin brought them together. Jarek's body ran cold. The feeling of being in danger escalated to the highest he had felt since arriving at the O'Connell mansion.

"What song would you like, Annie?" Martin asked her quietly.

"You already know my favorite song, Father," she replied.

Martin left Annie and Jarek standing there, holding each other. He went to the orchestra once again, directing them on what to play.

"This one is my absolute favorite Christmas song," Annie said to Jarek right as the music began.

The first few notes started and Jarek knew the song immediately.

"Ah, 'Carol of the Bells.' One of my favorites, too," Jarek said as he began to lead them in a Viennese waltz.

"Father is right, you know," Annie said to Jarek as they danced.

"Right about what?"

"You haven't been able to solve anything yet."

"Is that so? Am I not meeting your family's expectations?"

"I like you, Mr. Videni, but frankly, you have been a disappointment."

"Interesting . . ."

Jarek's lungs seemed to grow heavier and heavier and the room began to dim slightly. The dark shadow began to move in once again.

"Well, Miss Annie, you are very beautiful young lady. You could go places in this world. You clearly are smart, and that knowledge you have been consuming recently seemed to expand your mind. But frankly, I am a little disappointed in you as well."

Annie tightened her grip on Jarek's hand. "Is that so, Mr. Videni? And how have I disappointed you?"

"Well, you were clever for a while, but I have figured you out."

The song began its crescendo.

Jarek leaned in close to Annie's ear. "I know what you did. I know you are responsible for the killing of your own mother."

Annie's eyes gave a look of absolute terror to Jarek. Her pupils grew large. "That is absurd, Mr. Videni. I did no such thing."

Jarek twirled her. "Oh, Miss Annie, you can't hide it. And I know you planned to ensure my silence tonight, too."

Annie tried to let go of Jarek, but he strengthened his grip on her hands and continued the dance.

"You aren't the only one that has gifts, Miss Annie. In fact, because of what you did, my gifts are growing greatly. Because of what you did to the people in order for you to gain such abilities, they were more than happy to disclose your dealings."

"You're insane, Mr. Videni, and greatly mistaken," Annie said. Jarek could see some tears coming down from under her mask.

"No, Miss Annie, you just underestimated me."

The two continued to dance for the last bit of the song. When it came to its end, Jarek released his grip and Annie ran out of the ballroom, the double doors slamming behind her. Martin stood staring at Jarek.

"What's wrong?" Martin asked as Jarek moved toward him.

"I'm sorry, Martin, but it's her. It's Annie."

Jarek's shoulders began to slouch from the weight of the darkness in the room. He put a hand on Martin's shoulder, giving it a squeeze while looking at him. Martin's eyes began to well up with tears. Jarek looked around the room, realizing it was just the orchestra, Martin, and himself in the room. He assumed Rose must have the staff busy cleaning or had sent them home for the night.

"I am sorry, everyone, but it is time for you to leave," Martin said with a shaky and cracking voice.

"I need you to get out now. You all must go for the night. All of you," Jarek instructed them.

"But what . . ." one of the young men in the orchestra began to ask before Martin interrupted.

"He said to go. You can come back another day for your instruments and other belongings," Martin said in slightly raised voice.

Jarek began to sweat profusely. He could tell Martin's head was spinning and that he was even feeling the heaviness of the room.

The musicians began to move fast, clearing themselves out. As the house emptied, it grew heavier and heavier. The presence of the darkness was expanding and beginning to take a stand.

Jarek could see the dark shadows overtaking every corner, every nook and cranny. He began to see other shadows and entities starting to manifest through the ballroom. The dark being was attracting other spirits, other beings already torn between the world of the living and the dead.

Martin grabbed Jarek's arm. "Jarek, are you sure? How . . . how could it be Annie?"

Jarek placed his arm around Martin, who was on the brink of a breakdown. "Martin, I am sure, and I now know how she did it. Come, we must go find her. There is a darkness on this house and it's growing stronger. If we move quickly, we can still save Annie from it."

The men moved through the ballroom into the foyer. The last of the workers were scrambling to get out fast, clearly aware something was wrong.

Jarek's eyes darted all around. The darkness was seeping through the walls and through the cracks in the floor. He could see it, feel it, and smell it. Shadows darted all around in the distance; the darkness was attracting every foul spirit nearby.

The convocation of dark energy from the beings in one area was too much. Jarek felt like he was hardly able to breathe. He was continuing to sweat heavily. Jarek scanned the room and saw countless shadows and beings in all forms being drawn in. Spirits of the dead, gruesome and foul beings trying to attach themselves back to the world of the living. The darkness had grown to cover every inch of the home.

"What the hell is that?" Martin shouted.

Jarek realized even Martin could see some of the spirits. The energy in the house was overwhelming Jarek's senses. The electric lights in the house began to flicker. Then light bulbs began to explode from the energy overload. The drapes on the windows were moving about as if a strong breeze was blowing through the home. Yet the air itself was heavy and still.

Martin was nearly in a state of shock and stopped Jarek halfway up the stairs. "What is happening?"

"We must go upstairs, Martin. Your daughter is summoning the demon's full presence in defense of herself."

"What on earth are you talking about?"

"She thinks she has power over it! She doesn't know that the demon is only using her. It will kill her and anyone in its path in order to maintain a foothold in this world."

Martin stared blankly.

"Martin, come before it's too late." Jarek grabbed his hand and pulled him up the stairs.

The dark shadows moved up the stairs closely in tow, like a dark fog rolling in before a storm.

The men ran down the hallway toward the door to the library. As they came through the opening, they both stopped in their tracks.

The room was filled with noise and a building pressure. The furniture seemed to have been pushed to the edges, making a large open area in front of the staircase. In the center of the opening was the seal of the demon, the one Jarek had confirmed in the book. In the center of the seal was a chair with Rose sitting in it, hands tied behind her back and mouth gagged with her own handkerchief. The seal was created in blood, and Jarek could see that Rose's wrists were cut, blood oozing out. She was in pain, tears rolling down her cheeks.

Annie was at the top of the stairs kneeling down, eyes closed and muttering to herself.

"Annie, don't!" Jarek yelled.

"What is she doing?" Martin asked.

The room was growing so loud, as if a train were passing through. Drapes blew about, and the chandelier swayed from the dark energy.

"She's summoning it!"

Both men were frozen in their tracks, unable to move.

"Summoning what? I don't understand."

"Your daughter did it all, Martin. She has been learning about the dark arts behind your back. She thinks it's a gift, but it's all a trap. Demons twist the mind. She has been manipulated."

"Demons?" Martin exclaimed.

"Yes, Martin!"

Just then, the entire seal went up in bright blue flames. Jarek could no longer see Rose behind the brightness. Then the flames vanished as quickly as they appeared, leaving the seal intact but burned into the floor. Rose sat at the center motionless, but she didn't look any more harmed then previously.

"You're too late," Annie yelled down.

"Too late for what?" Martin asked, still confused about was unfolding before his eyes.

In a flash, the room became still. The air was heavy and dark. The demon's seal began to glow.

Silence, total silence.

Jarek looked at Martin. "He's coming."

CHAPTER 14

NOISOME

December 25, 1924, 12:29 a.m.

The library seemed to be frozen in time. Everything was silent. Jarek could only hear himself breathing. The darkest shadow Jarek had ever seen began to roll into the room from every direction, very slowly. The only light that remained was an unearthly glow from the demon's seal on the floor in the center of the room. It was a blue glow that matched the flames from earlier.

Suddenly the seal cracked right between where Rose was still motionless in the chair and Jarek. A loud whooshing sound began to come from the crack as the same dark shadow started seeping out in a twisted way.

Jarek realized that though he had felt and seen this dark being since his arrival, it had not fully crossed over into this world. Beings from the other side have the ability to only cross over as portions of themselves. Jarek had seen this in the many spirits he encountered throughout his life. People who have died are able to manifest parts of themselves in this world, either because they had not fully crossed over themselves or because they had something to finish in this world. Inhuman spirits are able to do the same, but they are able to manifest in this world much easier than a human spirit.

This full manifestation of the inhuman spirit was happening right before Jarek's eyes. As the black mist billowed from the crack in the floor, Jarek looked at Martin, who was in shock, and then he looked up at Annie, who was smiling.

"I told you. You were too late. I called on him and he is here," Annie said while looking down at the men still frozen in place.

"Annie, how could you? Why would you do this?" asked Martin, finally breaking his silence.

"Don't you see? Mother taught me bits about the world beyond our own. I just happened to find the information she was keeping from me from others, and then I was shown how to use it to my benefit."

"I . . . I don't understand," Martin replied.

"She thinks she can control this darkness and have it do her bidding in this world," Jarek said to Martin. "But the truth is, she has no idea what she is doing!"

"Oh, you foolish man. I know—"

"I am no fool," Jarek interjected. "I know that you pulled Samuel back to this world just so you could bind him to this house. I know that you coordinated with a poor drunk to kill your own mother to conjure the demon using her heart. And I know that you think the demon will grant your wishes. That it somehow makes you stronger. But you are wrong, Annie! You are very wrong!"

Jarek began to feel pressure building within his head, and there was a slight humming noise that started to build louder and louder. Everyone placed their palms on their temples. Even Rose began to move a bit as she was starting to regain consciousness. Jarek began to focus on another noise that started behind the humming. It was breathing . . . he could hear something breathing. A heavy and deep breathing. Jarek realized this wasn't an audible sound, but rather just in his head, all of their heads. Anyone passing by on the street would not have heard it, but everyone in this room could.

"What is that noise?" Martin asked.

"He's almost here!" Annie said as she got off her knees and raised her hands in the air.

"It's the demon," Rose said as she fully regained consciousness. "Why did you do it, Annie? Why are you making my Samuel suffer more?"

"What are you saying? I had no choice!"

"She needed to entice the demon when she conjured it using Sarah's heart," Jarek answered. "She is using Samuel's soul for it to feed. If a soul is available, the demon will come."

"How could you kill your mother?" Martin said shaking.

"She didn't," Jarek answered. Jarek looked directly up at Annie. "However, she arranged for it to happen. She didn't have the heart to do it herself."

Annie looked down at Jarek with fury in her eyes.

"What? Poor choice of words?" Jarek asked, trying to get Annie into a fit of pique.

"How dare you make a mockery of my abilities," she responded, clearly irritated.

"I did no such thing. I didn't mock your abilities, I simply questioned them," Jarek said. He was continuing to irk her in order to distract her.

Rose shot a look over to Jarek that seemed to ask him what the hell he was doing. To which he gave slight nod to settle her nerves.

"My abilities should not be questioned. I have grown in my gifts so much that I have been able to not only bring a spirit from beyond to our world, but I also bound it here and now I am able to summon a great being to help give me even more strength."

"Why would you even want that?" asked Martin. Tears were rolling down his cheeks, with sweat dripping down his forehead.

"Don't you see? I will be unstoppable. This world is not designed for people like me, Father. People like Mother, even. Don't you realize she was a joke to everyone? Anyone who is different in this world is mocked and ridiculed so much. With this power, I can begin to change that. I can live my life how I want to live it and get whatever I want, when I want."

The noise in the room grew so loud that Jarek could barely hear the last few words Annie spoke. Then the figure growing before him began to take its true physical shape.

Martin's expression grew wide. Annie, still standing with her arms in the air, now had a large grin on her face with eyes dark as night.

Slowly, the creature was becoming whole. After a few moments, it was there in the library, in its full true form.

The figure stood nearly seven feet tall, obstructing Jarek's view of Rose and the staircase. It stood like a man. The skin looked smooth initially, but as Jarek focused his eyes, he could tell it was cracked. No, not cracked—scaly. Its skin was dark gray, like charcoal. Jarek recognized its long fingers with yellowed claws immediately. Then he noticed that curled around the demon's right forearm and resting in its hand sat a viper. The face of the demon was boney, with harsh features. Lips even darker gray than the skin. Nose sharp, defined, and grotesque.

Then, while facing directly toward Jarek, the demon opened its cruel yellow eyes, nearly matching the color if its claws. The center of its eyes were like gaping holes, the darkest black that Jarek had ever seen.

The room fell silent once again.

"Demon, I have summoned—" Annie began to say, but the demon raised its left arm and quieted her. Then it brought its arm down, and Annie fell to her knees.

The demon did not break eye contact with Jarek, not a single blink. Then it took its left arm and gestured to the chair Rose was tied to. She slid to the edge of the seal and tipped over, her bindings and the chair breaking. Rose was released and stood up off to the side.

Everyone stood around the seal facing this creature from hell. Jarek at the top point of the pentagram of the demon's seal, Rose at the point to the right of Jarek, and Martin at the point to his left.

The silence was so unnerving that no one dared speak. The air remained heavy and stale, and an underlying stench burned Jarek's nostrils.

Jarek exchanged glances with Martin, who was looking to him for guidance. Then Jarek looked at Rose, and she exchanged a slight nod, indicating that she was all right and knew what was about to happen.

Jarek looked back at the demon. It had not stopped staring at Jarek, as if trying to read his mind. Then Jarek felt pressure in his head again, just as he had earlier. The demon began to speak in Jarek's mind. It didn't move its mouth or even change its facial expression.

"I am the mighty duke. I ruleth forty legions of spirits. I know all past, present, and what is to come. I can discover all secrets. I know why each spirit fell. I can make men wonderfully knowing in all things."

"I know exactly who you are, demon," Jarek said sternly while looking directly into its eyes.

Jarek noticed in his peripheral vision that everyone in the room was able to hear the demon in their minds, not just him. He could tell by their facial expressions as the demon spoke.

Then the demon opened its mouth to speak audibly. The unbearable breath from its mouth burned Jarek's lungs. Jarek quickly brought his arm up over his face to block the stench.

"You are nothing, Jarek Videni. Others fear your potential, but I do not. You are scum of the earth."

With one motion of its arm, the demon made all three of them drop to their knees.

"You're wrong, demon. In fact, you should fear me."

The demon gave a small crude laugh.

"Do you know why you should fear me, demon?" Jarek asked arrogantly.

"Why would I fear a small bug beneath my foot?"

Jarek began to stand up, clearly struggling. "Because, demon, I know who you are. I know your name. You know what that means, demon."

It stood still.

"You do not know of what you speak, boy," it said in its harsh voice.

"Rose, Martin. I need you now. This is the time for you to muster all your will and call out to the loved one you lost. We need their energy here tonight."

Martin looked worried and confused as he stared back at Jarek. Rose immediately stood tall and proud. She brought her head down slightly with her eyes closed and hands folded, almost as if she were praying.

"Fools!" the demon said.

It tried to take a step forward but seemed to be held in place at the center of the seal.

A gust of air moved through the room, making the curtains waver and a few items on the bookshelves fall.

Jarek remained standing, and Martin got off his knees and stood up.

"No! No!" Annie suddenly said from up at the top of the stairs as she realized what was happening.

"What . . . what can I do?" Martin asked.

"Martin, do as I said. Take all your energy within you to call out to Sarah. We need—"

"She is dead," Annie yelled.

"Martin! Call to her," Rose said from the other side of the seal without opening her eyes.

Martin saw Rose on the other side of the demon and mimicked exactly what she was doing.

"You pathetic beings. There isn't anyone here strong enough to release my grip on this house." The demon's voice echoed in the room.

A tactic Jarek assumed was to intimidate them. "Reach out! Reach out from your very core," he instructed.

Small sparks in the air began to manifest and swirl, the heaviness of the demon's presence mitigated slightly.

The demon began to laugh as the sparks grew brighter and larger.

Jarek began to speak. "I exorcise thee, o creature of hell, by the divine through whom—"

"No!" Annie began to yell again from atop the stairs. She seemed frozen in place, too.

The demon began to breathe heavy in anger, letting out a snarl like a dog.

Jarek paused in fear of not knowing his own abilities, distracted by all of the commotion in the room. Then a book from the shelves flew directly at him. He was able to dodge it, but he began to worry more. His forehead dripped in sweat. Jarek took a deep breath, closed his eyes, and reached within.

"Keep going, Jarek," came a voice.

Jarek's inner tenacity began to regrow as he saw the room in full. He was out of his body. He saw his own head bowed and his eyes shut. Each point of the pentagram contained the remaining strength he needed to banish the creature. Martin stood to his left and Rose to his right. Between the demon and the staircase at the furthest two points, Jarek saw Sarah and Samuel both manifested, completing the points of the star. Jarek opened his eyes, looked directly at the demon, and he began to cast the demon out.

"I exercise thee, o creature of hell, by the divine, through whom all things have been made."

The demon was resisting, and the room once again was growing louder and louder.

Jarek had to nearly yell the words. "So that every kind of phantasm may retire from thee and be unable to harm or deceive in any way through the invocation of the most high creator of all." Jarek stopped talking.

The demon continued looking directly at him. The viper dropped from its hand. It slithered on the floor toward Jarek. When the serpent reached the edge of the seal, it was unable to leave the circle. It slowly coiled up with its head raised, looking directly at him, as if ready to strike.

"You fool. I told you, you have no power here. Just leave this place before it's too late," the demon said while laughing.

Jarek observed the people here to help him, the living and those from beyond the veil. He closed his eyes and felt the energy begin to run through his veins, through every part of his body. The energy began to fuel that ember within. His confidence began to grow. Jarek took a deep breath, allowing it to fill every cell in his body.

Jarek opened his eyes. The room grew still. Silent once again.

The demon's attitude changed, clearly losing its credence on maintaining control of the situation. It was exhibiting a false smile, showing its gruesome teeth, in an attempt to demean Jarek's abilities.

Jarek smiled. "Let's try this again, Astaroth," Jarek said.

The demon's smile quickly disappeared as soon as Jarek spoke its name.

"I exorcise thee, o creature of hell, by the divine, through whom all things have been made, so that every kind of phantasm may retire from thee and be unable to harm or deceive in any way, through the invocation of the most high creator of all."

The demon's seal once again burst into flame. The coiled serpent burned to ash, letting out a loud hiss as it disappeared.

"No! Stop it!" Annie was yelling in the background as the demon began to lose its form. "Father, stop! Rose, how could you do this to me?"

Jarek continued. "Go back to hell, you vile creature. I know your name, and that gives me power over you. Go back to the pit from whence you came, Astaroth!"

The room began to seem like it was spinning. The air was whirling, and the sounds grew so loud, as if they were caught in the middle of storm. Thunder cracking, items banging, and noise from the deep protruding from the crack. Fire began to invert within the seal, crawling toward the center, beginning to consume the demon's body.

The humming Jarek heard in his head when the demon was entering the room earlier began once again, growing louder and louder. The demon began to turn into a thick heavy mist once again. An ungodly, almost squealing noise began to fill the room. Jarek, Martin, and Rose all covered their ears and crouched down to try and bear the unearthly noise.

The room continued to spin, objects from the shelves flying in all directions, and the curtains nearly ripping from the rods they hung from. Jarek felt a hard punch and sharp pain as a lamp from the side table flew across the room and broke across his back.

Jarek looked up in reaction to being struck and saw Astaroth fading away. Then, through the demon's mist, he was able to see the threads that pierced Samuel's lips break. The young man looked at Jarek and gave a slight nod and smile. He then looked at Rose, their eyes met.

"Know that I am sorry, and that I love you," Samuel said just before he vanished to the beyond.

Jarek's eyes shifted as he could see Sarah manifested fully, looking at Martin. She then turned her gaze toward Jarek, smiling. She was at peace. He gave her a small smile back and nodded his head. She then vanished in the same manner that Samuel had.

Jarek's eyes were watering from the air blowing throughout the room, but he also had a few tears rolling down his face out of gratitude toward those who had helped him, and he was in awe of everything happening before his eyes. He looked back toward the demon's seal. He saw the final bits of the beast seep away. Then the flames stopped.

Silence.

Jarek looked around from his crouched position. The room was still, the curtains were hanging still on their rods, objects were strewn about the floor. The moon outside gave the room just enough light for Jarek to see Martin and Rose lifting their heads up as well.

Martin stood up and walked across the room toward the door. He turned on the light switch, allowing the few remaining electric lamps to light.

The demon was gone, the only remaining portion of him being the marks of his seal, forever burned into the wooden floor.

"Where, where is Annie?" asked Rose as she turned her head, looking around the library.

"Annie! Annie!" Martin shouted.

Jarek looked toward the hidden door to the passageway. It was slightly open. He ran over to it and peered inside. He could see into his own room because that doorway was left open as well.

"She must have run out while Astaroth was banished," Jarek said.

"But where would she have gone?" Martin asked with a shaky voice.

"She couldn't have gotten far. We should search the house," Rose said.

"We can look. However, I am sure we won't find her," Jarek said.

"Why do you say that?" Martin said with tears in his eyes.

"She feels humiliated—by us catching her off guard and by the demon itself. She thought she'd be able to control it for her benefit. Blood summoning though is something no person should ever dabble in. It is a dark practice used by dark beings to manipulate and twist people. Their only intent is to bring more dark beings into our world."

"I am still confounded about this whole thing. I have so many questions," Martin said, taking a deep breath. "What, what all happened? This whole thing? The things I saw?"

Jarek looked at Martin, already knowing that these questions would be asked. He walked over to the sofa and grabbed one of the chairs that was tipped over and set it upright. "Martin, Rose, please sit. I will answer anything I am able to."

Rose moved toward the sofa and sat down. Martin slowly walked over to a globe on a stand. He opened the globe to reveal a few decanters and glassware. After pouring three cognacs, he handed one to Jarek and one to Rose. Then Martin sat down next to Rose on the sofa. He was clearly still incredibly shaken.

The three of them sat there in silence for a moment, taking sips of their much-needed drink. They all looked exhausted and in shambles. Clothes somewhat tattered, hair a mess, and faces still flushed.

Finally, Jarek broke the silence.

"Well, I think it is best to start at the beginning of what I have found to be the truth. Your wife, Sarah, was a gifted medium, Martin. She had talent and she wanted to push more of her limits to see her true potential. In all of her work, she began to find literature on all aspects of spiritualism, and some of that led to her acquiring books on some dark magic. I don't believe she ever intended to use it, merely gain more knowledge of it.

"Annie, being a curious young woman, began to move on from her normal books in the library and found Sarah's books. I believe that Annie felt called to learning this dark side of spiritualism. It might have been someone suggesting it to her, or it could have been the dark beings calling to her from the other side of the veil, or it may have just started as a dalliance with a subject seen as taboo.

"Annie began to dabble in the darker arts. She tried contacting spirits from the other side. I believe that she sensed Samuel had some natural gifts, too. Sarah had found Samuel to be sensitive to the spirit world, and she had been trying to keep him from being too exposed, so Annie talked to Samuel in secret about her own findings.

"Well, when Samuel was heartbroken after being rejected by his longtime friend Hamish, the only way he knew to ease his pain was by killing himself. Annie was devastated because Samuel was her only true friend.

"Rose, I am sure you were lost in your own grief and did not notice Annie's spiraling down the dark path. Martin, this tragedy was a triggering effect on your double consciousness, too, which I am sure made it difficult for you to focus on Annie during this time. You are aware of the medical condition that you are learning to work through, so you become a recluse when you worry you might become Peter in front of others. The fact though, Martin, is that this is a legitimate medical condition. Don't try to hide it and go through it alone. Instead, work through it and embrace the hands of friends when they are offered."

Jarek reached over and pat Martin on his knee. Martin nodded his head in agreement with what Jarek had said. A few tears rolled down Martin's cheeks.

Jarek continued. "I believe that Annie tried to use her newfound knowledge to try and bring Samuel back. She asked Hamish to help her try to summon Samuel's spirit here. Well, Annie was able to bring him here, but she is not a medium. She was unable to talk to him because Samuel wanted to move on, and she wasn't strong enough to commune with him once he was in our world.

"So Annie used even darker knowledge. Something or someone showed her the way. She found a way to summon a demon here to help grow her powers. She needed an innocent heart to start the process and an innocent soul for it to feed from. Annie had planned to lure Hamish back to the home and use his heart. However, he refused to see her because he was still shaken from the night they contacted Samuel.

"Sarah found out what Annie was up to, and Annie had already assumed Sarah would be angry with her and spoil the whole plan. What Sarah didn't know is that Annie had an alternative. She had already manipulated a poor drunk, Michael Stafford. Coincidently, I met this man when I first arrived in Saint Paul. Though I did not know his connection to here until recently. Annie had this man ready and waiting in the passageway over there the night she planned Sarah's death," Jarek said, gesturing.

"And Annie had already completed everything she needed to start the summoning process. Everything except for the heart. Sarah tried to confront Annie, but Annie stormed out of here. Sarah sensed Samuel, and she was able to commune with him and bring him here fully before the demon's presence began to grow. That is when Michael Stafford had come out of the passageway and stabbed Sarah. Samuel became bound to this house as the man cut Sarah's heart out and fed it to the demon's seal. In trying to help Samuel, Sarah's gifts ended up luring the demon here, allowing the binding process to occur.

"The demon's presence did give Annie more strength, allowing her to mask herself from having any part of this. With a demon's presence, a person is able to amplify their own abilities."

"So how then did you know it was her? How were you able to discover all this, Jarek" Rose asked.

"There were several things, to be honest. Mostly picking up on clues around the home. I conducted a Tarot reading when I first arrived to help me gauge the home and all the people and spirits in it. The reading allowed me to know where to focus my energies, and later on, it was actually Samuel who helped me ensure I was on the right path. Also, Sarah allowed me to see her memory of that fateful night as best she could. Though her memory was hazy due to the demon's power.

"I immediately was pulled toward Annie as the one responsible, but the dark forces drawn to this home, because of the demon, worked their hardest to throw me off her trail. But I continued to listen and see and feel. Then the answer was right before my eyes. Plain as I see you now."

"I . . . I still just don't understand, Jarek. How could you know?" Martin asked.

"I am an intuitive, Martin, and I have a connection to the other side. My grandmother helps me with that part. I just didn't realize how strong that connection was until I came here."

The chimes in the grandfather clock in the foyer began to ring. The three sat in total silence listening to how many chimes sounded. Jarek turned his head and looked out the window. The early morning still dark.

Six chimes rang.

"It's Christmas morning," Jarek said quietly.

"I have never felt so many emotions at once," Martin said. "I am confused by how this could all transpire in my very home. I have some comfort in gaining a bit of closure on Sarah's death, but I am sorrowful that I may have lost Annie now forever. It may be Christmas, but it is far from a merry one."

"Come, let us get some rest for a bit," Rose said while standing up.

"No, I actually should be leaving. I have some contacts I can reach out to and begin to search for Annie," Jarek said as he stood.

"She likely will try to find others like her, to find people open to the dark side of spiritualism."

Martin followed suit in standing before saying, "I owe you so much already, Jarek. However, I would appreciate any help you can provide in finding Annie."

Jarek gave Martin a small smile, trying to give him hope for Annie and her future.

"At least let me prepare some food and coffee for you to have before you leave," Rose said. "That way, you can freshen up and pack your bags."

"That is an excellent idea, Ms. Smith. I am a bit hungry."

The three began to walk out of the library. Rose first, then Jarek. Martin halted at the doorway, looking at where Sarah took her last breath. He turned back toward the hall where Jarek and Rose were standing.

"What about the man who actually killed Sarah? He must be held accountable," Rose said as all three began to walk down the hall.

"That man has paid his dues. He is dead now. Crushed by the lift while he was repairing it at the train station," Jarek responded with sadness in his eyes. Never would he have guessed the first spirit he met in Saint Paul was partially responsible for so much pain.

"That is a bit of comfort to know her killer has paid his debt, but also sort of sad, too," Martin said.

"It is all sad," Jarek said as he stopped at his bedroom door. "I'll see you downstairs in a bit.

"See you soon," Martin said, patting Jarek on the shoulder.

ЖК

Jarek walked down the stairs to the foyer. He could smell the buttery toast and coffee on the table, making his stomach rumble. Rose was just about to walk into the parlor when she turned toward Jarek.

"You can set your stuff right there, Mr. Videni. There is a spot of food and coffee ready for you. I need to go and light the fireplaces to try and warm up the home a bit more."

"Excellent," Jarek responded as he set his suitcase and satchel down, laying his coat and hat on top.

Jarek walked into the dining room to see Martin sitting at the table in silence. He sat down at the plate prepared for him. He then reached over and poured himself a cup of coffee.

Jarek knew Martin didn't want to talk at the moment. He was still processing everything that had transpired. The two men ate their small breakfast and drank their coffee in silence.

"Martin, I am going to be on my way now," Jarek said as he wiped the last bit of bread crumbs from his mouth with his napkin.

"I know, Jarek. Again, I just can't thank you enough. You are a much better man than I am," Martin said, holding back the tears wanting to return.

"Martin, I have watched you since coming here. I have heard from Rose, Samuel, and Sarah on what an amazing father and provider you are. You have built upon the business created by your father, turning it into one the most successful printing factories in the entire Midwest. You have built this home, always welcoming every person who crosses that threshold. With Sarah, you created a beautiful family. Yes, Annie is gone right now and is deeply disturbed, but I have hope. For you must always keep that ember of hope burning. She will be found, Martin. I will try to find a way to bring her back to the light. Her very soul was violated by the darkest of beasts, but I know that she will be able to pull through this with grace and go on to live an extremely successful life.

"Martin, you took Samuel and me into your home. You helped Samuel grow into the young man he was before that darkness overtook him. You all lost him much too soon, but because of your care and grace, I believe you were able to have him with you longer than the world may have. This has been a tremendously dark year, but because of your strength, you provided a small light of hope through it all. I have so much to thank you for. I will continue to stand by your family's side, through any trials that life may put us all through."

The two men stood and embraced each other. They then made their way to the foyer, where Rose was waiting.

Jarek noticed she was once again wearing her long dark dress and her hair was up, looking the very same as when she answered the door a few days ago. Rose stood tall and proud, but behind it all, her shoulders looked heavy.

Jarek faced both Martin and Rose, resting a hand on each of their shoulders. He took a few breaths, knowing that it was time for him to leave this home. "Martin, Rose, this year has been filled with much loss, confusion, and grief. It will take time for you to process and overcome. Remember, you can always reach out to me. I am only a telegram or letter away."

"Thank you, Jarek . . . for everything," Martin replied.

Rose stood silent, then brushed away a tear slowly rolling down her cheek.

"It will be all right, Rose. Go find Hamish. Help build each other up. Bring him into your family."

Rose acknowledged what Jarek was saying by nodding her head slightly, still unable to muster up any words for fear of crying. Jarek knew she was truly grateful for his help during this time and that she would ensure Hamish was looked after.

"You can now move forward with the courage and hope that was forged in tragedy," Jarek said with a gentle smile, acknowledging they had a long road to even a semblance of normalcy. "I will do my best in helping Annie. If anything of importance arises, I will be sure to send you information."

Jarek tightened his grip on each of their shoulders and pulled them in for a small gentle hug. As they all stood there in the foyer, the doorbell rang.

All three simultaneously looked at the door, unsure of who could be out on the stoop.

Rose walked over to open the door, revealing the young telegram messenger boy who frequently brought messages to Martin for the business.

"Merry Christmas, ma'am," the boy said.

"Merry Christmas, young man. How may I help you?" Rose asked.

"I hate to bother you on Christmas morning, ma'am, but I have a telegram," the boy said. "It is for a Mr. Videni. Does he live here, too?"

"That's me. I have been staying here," Jarek responded as he walked over to the doorway, perplexed, and reached past Rose.

"Here you are, sir," the boy said as he handed Jarek the telegram. "Have a very merry Christmas!" he said as he turned and headed down the stairs.

"You as well," Jarek shouted back.

The boy gave a wave behind his head in appreciation as he got on his bicycle and slowly rode down the snowy walkway.

Jarek unfolded his telegram and began to read the words printed on it. His palms became clammy and moist, and his hands began to shake.

Chasing Shadows ~ Genesis

NEW YORK
JAREK VIDENI
28 ST CLAIR AVE ST PAUL MN

YOU HAVE AWOKEN STOP I CAN SENSE IT STOP TIME FOR NEXT OPPORTUNITY STOP FAMILY NEEDS HELP STOP POSSIBLE DEMON STOP ULRIKA JOHNSTON STOP DEADWOOD SD STOP

LEONA

Jarek finished reading the telegram, folded it back up, and tucked it into his jacket pocket. He turned toward Martin and Rose, completely red-faced with sweat beginning to form on his forehead.

"Mr. Videni, what's wrong?" Rose asked anxiously.

Martin walked over and put his hand on Jarek's shoulder, not saying a word. He just looked deep into Jarek's sharp crystal blue eyes.

"I . . . I have to go. I am sorry, but I have to go," Jarek replied. "I will contact you if I hear anything about Annie's whereabouts. Goodbye."

Jarek bent down to retrieve his coat and slid it on over his body. He secured his satchel, picked up his suitcase, and turned to head out the door, leaving Martin and Rose standing in the foyer speechless. Jarek rushed down the sidewalk, almost stepping on a stray cat. It hissed and ran out of the way, toward the statue of Pan.

The O'Connell mansion grew smaller and smaller in the background as Jarek began to walk hastily toward Saint Paul Union Depot.

Jarek's mind was running wild, his blood rushing and heart beating hard from what he had just read. As he continued his walk in the cold, he began to process the words.

Jarek passed the impressive cathedral. He could hear the choir singing "Silent Night" to the people gathered for Christmas Mass. Large snowflakes slowly drifting to the ground added to the beauty of this holiday morning. Though his mind was rushing, a calmness came to Jarek. He knew that everything would be all right. The small ember of hope smoldering within him since birth finally had its spark. That ember became a flame of hope and passion that he would continue to use to fuel his gifts so that he may defeat much more darkness in this world and help those who need it.

This was Jarek's genesis.

EPILOGUE

Martin and Rose stood there watching Jarek rush down the path. He nearly stepped on the stray cat that Rose would leave food out for. They stood for a few moments in total silence. Martin took a few steps toward the door, staring out and allowing the cold light breeze to come into the home, chilling his cheeks and causing them to blush. Rose stood a pace behind Martin with her hands held behind her back. She remained motionless as a figure quietly walked up behind her and placed an object in the palm of her hand.

"How interesting," Martin said out loud while shaking his head in bewilderment. "I wonder what that was about. So very odd. And you know, I never did ask him how he knew to come here to begin with," Martin said as he turned and looked at Rose. "Why do you suppose—"

Martin was stopped midsentence from the sharp stinging sensation in his neck. Rose made one swift slash with a knife straight across his throat. Martin grabbed his throat in vain as the blood poured from the wound. He dropped to his knees before completely collapsing on the foyer floor.

"I sent for him. I needed him," Rose said as she stepped over Martin's nearly dead body. She walked toward the door, the figure close in tow. "Ugh, you have no idea how long I have been waiting to do that. You overly joyous naive boy."

Martin took his last few breaths of this life before his eyes closed in eternal rest.

Rose walked down the front steps onto the snow-dusted walkway. She still carried the bloodied knife in one hand as she crouched down and picked up the stray cat that ran over to her in the other. "There, there, Felix," she said as she pulled the cat in tight. "Viktor, your plan is all coming to fruition. That man has many gifts. He is the one we need . . . No matter the cost." Rose looked down at the snowy ground.

"I know that price is high for you, Rose. The cost of losing Samuel is high, but it will be worth it. You understand it?" Viktor said.

"I do see it, Viktor. And besides, you assured me this is only temporary. I will see my boy again. However, I still do not know how you were able to hide all this from Samuel's spirit. He seemed to have known so much and helped Jarek along the way."

"Astorath's power helped to conceal what we did not want Samuel to see. If he had discovered what was truly transpiring, his love for you and your love for him would have been broken. We needed that love to help send Astorath back. The demise of the demon awoke Jarek fully. Also . . . I know it wasn't just Samuel helping Jarek. I am not sure how, but Leona has been helping him too," Viktor said.

"And Annie still has no clue about any of this. It is almost comical that she doesn't realize the pawn that she is. After teaching her so many things, she is still so stupid. Do you suppose she went where she was instructed to go?"

"She would be foolish not to. But Annie is not a priority now; we need to focus on finding it. Come, we must get ready for our travels." Viktor turned and walked back into the house.

Rose continued to pet the cat as it began to purr. She smiled. Rose stood and began walking back toward the house. "Time to clean up this mess, Felix. Then we have much to prepare before going on our trip. There, there. Don't worry, Felix. You'll be coming with."

Rose crossed the threshold into the home, closing the door behind her.

A passerby looked up at the magnificent house, admiring the grandness of the home as they continued on with their Christmas morning walk. They were totally unaware they just stared at a house filled with tragedy . . . darkness . . . sadness. But also, a house where an ember of hope ignited into a flame, a flame burning bright and ready to consume all in its path.

Zachariah Jones

About the Author

Zachariah Jones grew up in small town in Central Minnesota. He became fascinated with books at a young age. In fact, his fist job at the age of 14 was working in the local library. He was responsible for shelving books and repairing books. Zachariah felt called to serve in the armed forces where he has been serving since age 17. He is also a graduate of Saint John's University, and holds a degree in Political Science. He has toyed with writing for many years; however, he finally has taken the time to start turning the short stories he had into novels. His debut novel is the first book in a trilogy, *Chasing Shadows*.

Zachariah currently lives in eastern Minnesota in a small river town with his husband and dog. When Zachariah is not working, he enjoys anything outdoors, gardening, cooking, and spending time relaxing in his home.

Made in the USA
Middletown, DE
08 December 2022